WHEN SHE OPENED HER EYES AGAIN...

the look of pain and despair on Roen's face broke the camel's back. *This is ridiculous.* She couldn't take him lying alone every night when she loved him so much it hurt.

And now that horrifying, ominous feeling in her gut told her something bad was coming. Something that would separate them permanently.

God, she wanted to tell him, but how the hell would that help anyone? By making him paranoid or triggering a self-fulfilling prophecy?

Surprisingly, all her earlier apprehensions about being with him vanished, and she completely understood what he'd been trying to say earlier. There wasn't going to be a tomorrow or later. This was it for them. How, she didn't know. But God help her, she couldn't bear the thought of never knowing, or worse, deprive him of that memory if she were the one who didn't survive.

"This is torture, Liv. And I really can't handle it right now—I've got to go." Roen headed for the door.

Liv sucked back her heavy thoughts. "I changed my mind. I want to sleep with you," she blurted out.

OTHER WORKS BY MIMI JEAN PAMFILOFF

FATE BOOK (New Adult Suspense/Humor)
FATE BOOK TWO (New Adult Suspense/Humor)
HAPPY PANTS CAFÉ SERIES (Prequel)
(Romantic Comedy)

THE KING TRILOGY (Dark Fantasy)

King's (Book 1)
King for a Day (Book 2)
King of Me (Book 3)

THE ACCIDENTALLY YOURS SERIES
(Paranormal Romance/Humor)

Accidentally in Love with…a God?
Accidentally Married to…a Vampire?
Sun God Seeks…Surrogate?
Accidentally…Evil? (a Novella)
Vampires Need Not…Apply?
Accidentally…Cimil? (a Novella)
Accidentally…Over? (Series Finale)

COMING SOON

IMMORTAL MATCHMAKERS, INC. (Book 1)
(Paranormal Romance/Humor)
MERCILESS (Book 3, the Mermen Trilogy)
MACK (Book 4, the King Series) (Dark Fantasy)
THE HAPPY PANTS CAFÉ SERIES (Book 1)
(Romantic Comedy)

ISBN-10: 061567965X
ISBN-13: 978-0-615-67965-5

Cover Design: EarthlyCharms.com

Editing: Latoya C. Smith and Pauline Nolet

Interior design: WriteIntoPrint.com

And every time you illegally share or download a book, YOU ARE HELPING these people. Meanwhile, people like me, who work to support a family and children, are left wondering why anyone would condone this.

So please, please ask yourself who YOU are HELPING when you support ebook piracy and then ask yourself who you are HURTING.

And for those who legally purchased or borrowed or obtained my work from a reputable retailer (not sure, just ask me!) muchas thank yous! You rock.

Dedicated to Dalitza Morales.

Because you are completely mad.
(In a good way.)

MerMadmen

"There are only two mistakes one can make along the road to truth; not going all the way, and not starting."

—Buddha

Chapter One

With a terrified gasp, twenty-nine-year-old Liv Stratton's eyes flew open. *Oh God, where the hell am I?* She slowly sat up, her eyes searching the dark room for an answer. A large black rectangle sat on the wall ahead—a television. Off to the left, a dark hallway faded into blackness. To the right, drawn curtains covered an entire wall. Nothing, not even the cool air wafting over her bare breasts, seemed familiar.

Wait. Bare? She glanced at the sheet covering her naked body from the waist down. *Oh, crap. Did I go home with someone?* But that wasn't like her at all. She didn't do the drunk "hookup thing."

She shoved her hands into her tangled long hair. *Think, think, think. What's the last thing you remember?* But it was all a blank.

Hugging the sheet to her body, she sprang from the king-sized bed and whipped back the velvety white drapes. In the distance, beyond a patch of dark rolling hills sprinkled with lights, she spotted dozens of shimmering skyscrapers clustered around one tall structure shaped like the queen on a chessboard.

The Space Needle? She'd lived in Seattle the last few years, while doing her PhD in sociology at Washington State, so she knew the building well. *But how did I get—*

Her mind began filling in the blanks with images of her parents' anniversary party at their favorite restaurant in Wrangell, Alaska—her hometown. *But how did I get here?*

"Miss Stratton," said a deep, velvety smooth voice behind her.

Liv yelped.

In the darkened doorway across the room stood the large, menacing silhouette of a man she thought she'd never see again. He was a man of unspeakable beauty, dangerous as hell, and he'd once saved her life. But that didn't mean he was there to do it again. The last time they'd met, he'd made it clear what he thought of her: not much.

"Roen, what am I doing here?"

Wearing what looked to be a white dress shirt and dark slacks, he began unbuttoning his cuffs and rolling up his sleeves, like a man preparing for a little dirty work.

Liv would've stepped back, but back meant into the window.

"Why do *you* think you're here?" he asked, his voice exaggeratedly slow yet overtly menacing.

Given your tone? Can't be good.

Liv cleared her throat. "Did you really bring me here to play guessing games?"

"You speak bravely for someone so frightened."

"Who said I'm frightened?" she responded.

"I can see it on your face."

So he can see in the dark now. It wasn't a surprise given so much about Roen had changed. Once upon a time he'd been just a man. A billionaire who owned one of the world's largest shipping companies. Even then, however, his cutthroat tactics and icy heart had been as infamous as his looks—Sexiest Man of the Year. Regrettably, he'd only become more strikingly handsome. His caramel brown hair alone, with streaks of gold and chestnut, qualified him for the category of unspeakably beautiful. And those eyes. Lord, those eyes. A vibrant green with gold rings around the pupils. Every time he looked at her, his raw sexual energy left her feeling defenseless. At least, that's what she remembered thinking the last time she'd seen him with the lights on.

Liv tightened her grip on the sheet around her body. "Fine. I'm terrified, but can you blame me? I have no idea how I got here, and the last time we spoke, you told me to crawl back to my pathetic life. I also believe your hand was raised to slap me."

"How could I forget?" he said in an amused, sadistic tone. "You didn't flinch."

"Guess I'm not so weak after all, am I?" That had been what he'd called her: "weak," a trait he clearly loathed.

Roen laughed and crossed his thick arms over his chest. No doubt about it, the man's size was menacing—broad shoulders, hard muscles covering every inch, and six-six-ish in height. Yeah, he definitely looked like he'd grown an inch since she'd last seen him. Of course, grown men didn't usually get taller, but according to Roen, he and his men weren't exactly human. Then there was that water they drank to make them stronger. It dripped from the walls inside the giant cavern on the island they called home. The water, however, wasn't simply water; it was so much more. Just like that crazy island wasn't an island.

"I never would've hit you." He shoved his hands into his pockets as if holstering his weapons. "Nor did I mean those words. I was upset that day and had every right to be."

Maybe he did. She had broken a pretty big promise not to speak to anyone about his new home or its people, but all that was in the past now, and Liv desperately wanted to move on with her life. Or, more accurately stated, move on from him. Exactly like he'd asked.

If only my heart would let me.

"Let's cut the crap. Tell me why I'm here," she demanded.

Roen gestured toward the bed. "Why don't you sit down?"

Liv didn't budge.

"I insist," he said in a stern tone.

She wished he'd flip on the lights so she could see his expression more clearly. It might clue her in on what he intended to do to her. In his new world, the laws regarding a woman's place, purpose, and rights were fairly clear. And they were barbaric.

Liv shook her head no.

"Liiiv," he growled.

"Uh-uh." She shook a finger at him. "*You* don't get to tell me what to do. We are not on your island. And even if we were, I'd still tell you to pound sand. So whatever you have planned—whatever goddamned reason you brought me here, you can expect nothing but a fight from me."

Despite being all the way across the room, she felt the tension and heat radiating from his body. It made her skin tingle with the awareness of how much she missed his rough hands on her body. No one's touch compared to Roen's. No *man* compared to Roen.

Don't, Liv. Don't open your heart to him again. It didn't end well last time.

"I'm not here to hurt you, Liv. I'm here to warn you."

"You brought me all the way to Seattle, stripped me down naked, and put me in your bed, to *warn* me?" She didn't believe that for a moment.

"You can't go back to the island, Liv. I can't protect you this time."

"What the hell are you talking about?" She'd barely escaped with her life from that hellhole, and Roen knew it.

"Fucking listen to me, woman," Roen yelled, his voice a booming roar that bounced off the walls, hitting her from every direction. “They are coming for you. Don’t let them take you back!”

“What are you talking about?” Liv’s heart galloped inside her chest.

Roen’s head snapped up toward the ceiling, listening to something. “It’s already too late.” He looked back at her. “Fight, Liv. Kill them if you have to. But don’t let them get you on that island.”

“I don’t understa—”

Liv awoke in a pitch-black room, sweaty, panting, and tears streaming down her face. *Oh fuck. What’s going on?* Like her dream, only a sheet covered her naked body. Unlike her dream, this room was pitch black.

“I bet,” said a deep male voice, “you’ve got a lot of questions right now.”

A bright light flooded the room, and she sat up quickly, holding the sheet across her chest. Her eyes took more than a second to adjust, but there was no mistaking the man standing next to the closed door with his hand on the light switch.

Shane. Oh crap.

Seeing him did not fall anywhere near the “this is good” category, although his beautiful face, jet black hair, and striking green eyes might lead a woman to believe otherwise. But that was the thing about the men from the island of El Corazón; their male beauty transcended all logic and broke every rule in the universe. Men should not be so gorgeous. It wasn’t fair or natural. Not when they were equally dangerous and strong, nearly seven feet in height and ripped from head to toe.

A deadly combination. Especially if you were a woman and crossed paths with one.

Liv was about to ask where they were when she realized the cramped, stuffy room, with dark wood-paneled walls, swayed gently from side to side. *Shit. This can't be happening.*

"How the hell did you get me onto a boat?" She needn't ask where they were going. Godfuckingdammit, she already knew.

Shane flashed a cocky sinister grin and then casually plunked down in the navy blue armchair pushed into the corner only a few feet away. His enormous muscle-packed body stretched the fabric of his jeans and white T-shirt to their limits. "I'm a merman. We have our ways of getting things done."

Liv's mind still tripped every time one of these men said that word. Mermen weren't real. And the ones in storybooks had tails and scales. *Not these guys.*

"We become especially crafty," he added, "during the Collection. Which is exactly why you're here."

Oh shit. Roen once explained that the men from the island periodically went to the mainland and brought back women. The Collection. He said they came willingly—a law of theirs—but that wasn't the full story. Hell no. These men possessed persuasive powers over the female gender, like Pied Pipers of sex, and what they did with their "guests" once they got to the island was a travesty of the gravest sort.

But you're immune to them. No one knew why, but who cared? Once they arrived to that nightmare somewhere in the North Pacific, she'd find Roen, who now led this tribe of barbaric assholes, and tell him they'd brought her against her will.

While those thoughts sieved through Liv's head, she remembered her dream—Roen telling her to fight, that he couldn't protect her this time. But had that been real or her subconscious pushing her to wake the hell up?

Of course, it was a dream.

"Whatever you're thinking of doing, Shane, don't forget Roen is your leader. He'll pluck off your legs when he finds out what you've done."

"You mean, how I took you? Oh no. I'm so afraid." He laughed and wiggled his fingers in the air for effect. "Actually, Liv, you're the one he's going to be angry with. Not me."

"Why?"

He lowered his head and stared with a wolfish grin, putting her entire body into fight-or-flight mode. "Because you're going to tell him you want to fuck me, that you wanted me all along."

Liv's jaw nearly unhinged. He was out of his damned merman mind. Long story short, Liv had been staying on a fishing boat last March, observing the crew as part of her dissertation on human bonding and relationships. Tragically, a violent storm sank the ship and took the crew with it. Liv had been the only survivor, but after ten days adrift on a raft in open waters and out of drinking water, she'd been sure there wouldn't be a happy ending to her story. So when the island appeared out of nowhere along with Shane, she'd thought she'd been saved. Wrong. Shane made it clear that they—the men on the island—planned to keep her. And when she ran, he punished her for it, nearly drowning her. If Roen hadn't shown up on the island, looking for whatever he'd been searching for that day out at sea, Liv's life would've turned out drastically different. So would've Roen's. He'd had to fight for leadership—become one of *them*—simply to free her. All that said, Roen knew Liv hated Shane. She'd never willingly be with him.

"I don't think so, Shane. And Roen would never believe that anyway."

"I have a feeling you can be convincing when you want. And I have another feeling that when you tell him you're on the island of your own free will, aching to give your sweet pussy to me, he'll believe every word."

Hearing him say *that* word made her entire body revolt. He was disgusting and crude.

Then speak his language, Liv. Maybe he'll understand. "Go fuck yourself, Shane. I'm not yours. I never will be. Because I am absolutely, one hundred percent too good for you. Even my…" she paused to spit out the tactless words she hated saying, "my sweet pussy."

The room filled with a menacing vibe that gave off the faint smell of gunpowder.

Shane leaned forward, hands clasped, staring at her like a soulless shark. "Okay. If that's how you wish to play. I have other women to choose from on this ship."

Oh no. "How many did you shitty bastards take?"

He grinned proudly. "Roughly fifty, but the Collection is far from over. The island is demanding we keep going until every man—mated or not—has fathered a new child. The fucking won't stop until the goddess is appeased." He chuckled. "Damn, I love that island."

Everyone had a sore spot and this was Liv's: men victimizing women. In the women's shelter where she used to volunteer, she'd witnessed how these predators—disguised as loving husbands and boyfriends—took pleasure in breaking a woman's spirit. Usually they did it with beatings, but sometimes they did it with words. Either way, by the time the women made it to her, only the shell of who they once were remained.

What Shane and these men intended to do may not involve punching, but they did plan to rob these women of the lives they were entitled to.

"Think about what you're doing to them," Liv said. "Or to their families, who are wondering right now where they are."

"Why the hell would I care about a bunch of useless landlovers? Well, other than ensuring they'll make adequate caretakers for our offspring. By the way, your mother is lovely—like an older version of you. I thought about taking her, too, but she's a little old for raising mermen. I do like her quilting, though."

He'd been spying on her family? For how long? "You're a monster."

"No. I'm a merman. I take what little pleasures are granted to us. And occasionally getting laid is one of them." He winked.

"I guess since I was blessed with an immunity to your awesome mermanly charms, I'm going to have to decline any offers. Also, just to be clear, I'm not going to lie to Roen."

Shane stood up. "I think you will. I think you'll do everything I say. Because the woman I have in mind to replace you looks oddly similar—long dark hair, about your height, and beautiful brown eyes. In fact, you could almost be twins." He released an accomplished sigh.

Liv felt her blood pressure, heart, and soul crash into the floor. "You have Dana?" she whispered.

"Yes, I believe I do," he said happily. "She is your *baby* sister, isn't she? Not so innocent, but so very sweet and so very susceptible to our charms. In fact, she's up on deck right now with the other women, sipping margaritas with my men. It's a wild party."

Party. That word triggered a flash of memories. Liv had been at her parents' anniversary party at a restaurant overlooking the marina when her sister Krista—the oldest—told her a man had shown up claiming to be her date. Krista had described him as tall with short hair, overwhelmingly handsome, and built. Liv had thought and hoped he might be Roen, because dangerous or not, her heart still felt something for that man. Maybe it always would.

But, sadly, Shane had been waiting outside on that terrace. She didn't remember much else, but clearly more had happened. They now had Dana, her twenty-four-year-old sister, and they were on a goddamned boat heading back to that goddamned island no one knew existed, where they would be "claimed" in a bloody, barbaric ritual that defied all logic.

Liv's entire body shook with rage. "If you or any of your men touch her, I'll kill you. Do you understand me, Shane?"

"Ohhh…That's what gets me hard, little landlover. Your feisty attitude. I'm going to enjoy fucking you, Liv. Over and over again until our time is up."

"Roen will never let it happen." And neither would she.

"He will let it happen because he's a coward, and you'll do anything to make sure your sister goes free. Won't you, Liv?"

She looked down at the floor, holding back her fury and possibly every cuss word in the English dictionary.

"Wouldn't you?" he repeated threateningly.

"Let her go, Shane," she growled.

"I will. If you do what I ask." Shane reached for the door. "I'll have someone bring you clothes and food. Get some rest, Liv. You and your sweet little pussy are going to be needing it."

Liv glared at that vile, hideous man, thinking of her dream: "Kill them if you have to, Liv. But don't let them get you on that island."

Liv had never taken anyone's life—in her world it wasn't even a consideration—but to save Dana from what lay ahead, she wouldn't hesitate. And curse her to hell, but killing a sadistic predator like Shane? She might even enjoy it.

Chapter Two

Roen stood on the edge of a rugged cliff at midday, overlooking the never-ending ripples of blue ocean. The salty wind whipped through his hair and chilled his skin to a throbbing numbness. *I must jump. I must jump and save her.*

Down below, the crashing waves broke violently against the black volcanic rocks. If he jumped, he knew he might not survive.

But I have to save her. With every passing second, she drifted farther and farther away in her yellow life raft. It would be impossible to find her in such a big ocean if he didn't go after her now.

Roen flashed a glance over his shoulder, where his men stood in formation, awaiting their fates like sentinels from an ancient world.

"You cannot save them both, merman," said the island in that sadistic voice of a woman he'd come to know and loathe so well. *"You must choose: your mate or your people."*

"I will not choose," he screamed over the roar of powerful waves below. "I would rather die."

"You will choose or you will all *die."*

"Why are you doing this?" he screamed.

"Because no one disobeys me. And those who do pay the price."

"Mr. Doran, here's your coffee," said Cherie, Roen's personal assistant, snapping him out of his daydream—a repeat of his nightmare from the last two months. "Strong. Just the way you like it."

Sitting at his antique desk, he gave her a quick nod, masking his moment of disorientation. "Thank you."

Don't think anything of the dream—it's merely your subconscious blowing off steam. At least, that's what he hoped.

"You're very welcome, sir." Cherie flashed a flirty little smile before pouring him a cup. For the record, Cherie never used to smile, never showed emotion, but she did speak three dialects of Chinese, which was why he'd hired her a few years back. He hoped he wouldn't have to fire her now. After all, she'd done nothing wrong. He was the one who'd changed.

"I'll call you if I need anything further," Roen added to politely dismiss her.

A wounded expression flickered in her brown eyes before she stormed out the door of his corner office located on the twentieth floor of his headquarters in downtown Seattle.

Roen hissed out a breath and ran one hand through his chin-length hair. No question about it, life had become infinitely more complex. That included being around the opposite sex, which had been a distraction before he'd discovered—and accepted—who he truly was. What he truly was. But now, it was a goddamned nightmare. This morning in the elevator of his building, for example, a new tenant he'd seen only in passing threw her arms around him, shrieking she couldn't stop thinking about being together again. The security guard and doormen had to pry her reaching lips from his neck, and when they did, she began ranting, "You can't leave me! I need you!" behaving like they'd had a romantic breakup. He truly felt bad for these women because their lust was an illusion. In his case, his only desire was for the one woman he couldn't have: Liv. Day and night, he couldn't stop thinking about her—those wide brown eyes and long, silky, dark hair. Those sweet, plump lips and curvy body meant for touching. With every breath he took, his desire only grew. Gnawing, aching, throbbing for one whiff of her skin and a taste of the soft flesh between her—

Mind back to work, you arse. You can't have her. Well, technically he could, but it would destroy her in the process. It was simply what happened to women who got involved with his kind. He and his men were like poison. To the heart, the soul, and mind. He need only think of how his father destroyed his mother to remember that.

Roen begrudgingly turned his attention back to the stacks of papers on his desk when his phone rang.

Roen knew the number and hit speaker. "Phil, I hope you're calling with good news."

Phil, his lawyer in Chicago, made a grumbling sound. "No. Not today, because I've looked at this every which way. You're asking for the impossible."

"Impossible is you surviving the ass kicking I'm going to give you if you don't fucking figure this out." Roen picked up his mug and sipped his piping hot black coffee.

"God, you're such a prick. And is it my imagination, or has it only gotten worse? Like you went to prick finishing school to polish those sharp edges."

Actually, Phil's sarcastic remark wasn't far from the truth. Roen had changed. Physically, he was a bit larger now—a side effect of "becoming one" with his new home and people—but mentally, he had shed any soft edges. Not that he'd had many. *Now, even less.* Because the men of his kind, regardless of where they started out in life, only served one purpose: guarding that damned island. They were born to kill, defend, and fight.

Roen laughed. "You're lucky I like you, Phil."

"Flattered, I'm sure. But I really meant what I said, Ro."

Ro. Roen hated it when Phil used his nickname. It always meant bad news. "Phiiil," Roen warned. "Don't tell me it can't be done. You pay who you have to—senators, more useless lawyers, whothefokeever—to *foking* figure it out and make it happen."

"I can't do a *foking* thing to get you a *foking* title to your *foking* land if you don't *foking* tell me where the island is."

The "foking" remark was a jab at Roen's slight Scottish accent. He'd more or less grown up in the United States, but his roots tended to show when he got angry and swore—i.e., all the *foking* time.

Roen grumbled a few choice profanities under his breath before explaining for the tenth time, "I can't tell you where the island is yet. Not until I'm sure we'll get this approved." Otherwise, word would get out that there was an uncharted island in the middle of the North Pacific that had no legal owner. Every fucking idiot with a boat in this hemisphere would be looking for it. "Make something up—tell them we're waiting for surveyors or something."

"I'll do what I can, but this is going to take time. Years perhaps."

"Nope. It's got to happen fast." Roen was up against the clock on this. Every day he watched the despair in his men's eyes grow more toxic. For far too long, they'd been promised the return of the women they loved, only to be forced, blackmailed, and bullied by the island to protect her. Yes, she was alive—he'd spoken with her more than once and they could all hear her heartbeat. Yes, it was goddamned strange. But no stranger than the fact he now led the "people" who lived there. And certainly no stranger than being one of them—not quite human, and definitely not the half-fish creatures portrayed in old whaler legends. The island's "women," on the other hand, were an entirely different story, the very thing nightmares were made of.

"I'll do my best, Roen, but you might want to come up with a plan B, just in case."

"There is no plan B, Phil. This is the only option. Why do you think I'm going to all this trouble?" According to one of their scriptures, his people would soon turn on each other—those who were fed up with being prisoners versus those who believed protecting the island was their sacred purpose. Once the fighting started, many men would die and the island would become vulnerable to humans—landlovers, as they were called. Word would get out about the island's sacred water, a substance that cured any illness and prolonged life. But the island also needed that water to stay alive. It was her blood. Take too much or contaminate the island with too many humans, and the island would die. Unfortunately, the world would go with it because that water, which leached into the ocean and spread via the rain, served another purpose: It served as a catalyst to initiate a heartbeat in the very early stages of embryonic development. So without the island, all life would quickly wither.

All this was why Roen's plan had to be carried out properly. First, however, he had to prove to the island she didn't need them anymore. At least, not like before. In this day and age, there were far better ways to keep her protected from the landlovers.

"Money is no object," he said to Phil. "If it takes selling my company, I'll do it. This is important."

"Why? Do you plan to build a resort or a cruise ship port? Is that what this is about?"

"The island has been in my family for generations, and I want to legally pass it on to my heirs," he lied. Actually, he needed to hire private security to safeguard the waters, but that would mean public exposure. Holding a legal title to the land would prevent someone else from trying to stake a claim.

"Heirs?" Phil stifled a laugh. "Is the infamous bachelor Roen Doran settling down, or are we talking about the hordes of little bastards who will be coming forward with a claim?"

Children. Now there was a sore subject. Given the direction things were heading, it would be foolish to have children. But that was yet another of the many disagreements he had with the almighty island, who insisted now was a perfect time—a testament to her utter naïveté. She refused to accept that her way of doing things was driving everyone toward extinction. Unfortunately, she'd had the final word on the matter when he'd been forced to barter for Liv's freedom. Roen had to vow complete obedience to the island, forsaking any attachments his heart had to Liv—something he quickly learned might be impossible. Second, he had to agree to hold a Collection and fully participate. Yes, the island wanted him and every other man to get to work producing more mermen for her protection. He'd agreed; then he swore to himself that if they survived, the next generation of mermen would be free from this twisted cycle of indentured servitude.

And because there was nothing more important to him than Liv.

Liv. An image flashed in his mind of holding her naked, their sweat-slicked skin pressed together, her scent filling his nostrils and—

Stop torturing yourself. She's free now, and she'll never end up becoming one of those creatures or going mad like your poor mother. Find happiness in that.

He adjusted himself in his black slacks, something he found himself doing every time he thought about Liv, which was twenty times a day. Maybe more.

Because she's perfect. Her smile, her heart, her body with those soft pink—

"Roen? You still there?" Phil's voice snapped him away from yet another X-rated Liv fantasy.

Roen looked up at the ceiling and groaned. How much longer could he live like this? "Yes. I'm here."

"I want to help you, Roen, but even I—"

"You've never failed me once, Phil. So stop your *foking* whining and get me the title before I fly there and hurt you." Roen hung up the phone and turned his focus to the stack of presentations on his desk. He'd been meeting with defense contractors all week, getting proposals for equipment and, yes, weapons. Once that was figured out, a trust would be established so there would always be money to keep the island protected.

Roen's cell phone vibrated on his desk, and he glanced at the screen. It was Lyle, his younger brother by about two years.

"What's wrong, Lyle?" Roen said into the phone.

"You need to turn on the news." Lyle's deep voice was filled with dread.

"I hate surprises. Just tell me."

"Turn it on. Then get your ass home to the island." Lyle ended the call.

"Foke." Roen walked over to the small sitting area in the corner of his office and used the remote to turn on the flat screen. He never really watched the thing unless he wanted to monitor the market. Roen flipped through the channels. *Dammit. Where the foke is the bloody news?*

"Cherie!" he called out.

Within seconds, her head of long black hair peeked through the door. "Yes?"

"Where the hell is the news?"

She rushed over and took the remote. "There you go."

When the channel popped up, Roen felt like he might actually pass out. "No. Foking no."

It was a headshot of Liv and a similar-looking woman—dark hair and eyes, pale skin, and heart-shaped lips. The word "Abducted" flashed across the bottom of the screen.

"Do you know her?" Cherie asked.

Roen nodded absentmindedly while listening to the reporters. Liv and her younger sister, Dana, had been taken by a large, "noticeably handsome" man approximately seven feet in height, in the middle of a family gathering. The reporters noted that the case was of special interest due to Liv being the same woman who'd been lost at sea and miraculously rescued three months ago. It was a story that gained national coverage, primarily because it had been linked to his own disappearance. Obviously, he'd resurfaced.

Foke. This can't be happening.

Roen dropped his head. "Shut it off. Tell Edward to have my plane ready in ten minutes." Edward was one of *them*, since humans weren't generally welcome on the island, nor could they see it unless right on top of the damned thing or the island wished to reveal herself. The island had many, many impressive abilities, which he'd been taking the time to study.

Obviously, keeping her word isn't one of them. Rage pulsed through his body. He'd made a deal. A goddamned deal. *What is she up to?*

"Yes, Mr. Doran. Right away." Cherie clicked off the television and slowly rubbed his arm. "Are you sure I can't do anything for you?" she purred with lust-filled eyes.

Roen felt the rage building inside him over Liv. He cracked his neck and then straightened his tie. "No. Nothing."

"But, sir—"

"No! For *foke's* sake, Cherie. Now go the hell home!" he roared.

Cherie jumped in her skin and darted away, crying.

Oh, hell. He'd made her cry. But yelling had been a far better option than risking her getting hurt, considering he fully intended to break something. Dammit, it was his office. *And foking hell!* One of his own had taken Liv, likely as part of the Collection. So which one of his men had chosen to go after Liv? And why?

Does it matter?

Because Liv was his and only his. He'd be damned if he let some other merman fuck up her life. He'd done far too much, suffered far too much to keep her safe. *And I'll be damned if I let anyone touch her.*

Roen blew out a steady breath while his mind came to grips with the other unsavory elements of this situation. He was going in for a fight he couldn't possibly win. No, he didn't mean the other man—he'd squash the bastard—but then what? He would have to see Liv, be in the same room with her, and he knew he wouldn't be able to control himself this time. He wanted her more than he wanted to breathe.

If you take her, you'll be ending the woman you love. Roen balled his fists. Maybe that's what the island wanted. *Well, too foking bad. I won't allow anyone to hurt Liv.*

CHAPTER THREE

"I won't let you do this to her, Shane! Do you hear me? Let me out!" Every waking hour over three long days, Liv pounded the door to no avail. Sadly, being locked up by these aquatic lunatics had become a theme in her life. "Let me the fuck out!"

Liv was at her wit's end, her mind spinning in a protective rage knowing what would happen once they reached the island. Yes, she had escaped last time with a hefty sacrifice on Roen's part. Absurdly, part of that sacrifice was Roen's commitment to hold a Collection.

And why a Collection? It tied back to the fact that women only served two purposes in their world: making more warriors to protect their home during the day or being turned into horrid nocturnal sea creatures that patrolled the waters at night. Two armies. One purpose.

This episode of crazy fucked-up misogynist nightmares is brought to you by...the island. The island, because the human world isn't scary enough. Liv didn't know why she made jokes; the situation was anything but funny. Not for her, Dana, or any of the other women who'd either end up becoming monsters or mommies.

Yes, yes. Of course there were worse fates than having a baby—all male, by the way—with a stranger who wasn't exactly human and being left alone to raise it. The real tragedy came later when the child grew, only to become another slave to the island. No way was that a happy ending for these women, who'd be kowtowed by whatever powers the mermen held over females and then brainwashed into having sex.

Oh, God. Sex... Liv's mouth went dry. Roen would probably be on that island. Roen—tall, hard, likely shirtless, definitely rippling with powerful muscles and bronzed skin—Roen. And she'd be forced to look at him, dammit. Including that beautiful face with those soft, slightly full, sensual lips and a strong jaw covered in short rich-brown whiskers. She'd have to gaze into those fierce, exotic, green-and-hazel eyes while her senses bathed in his delicious, spicy masculine scent. He would rouse the cruelest of carnal urges deep inside, only to leave her wanting. And then there was her heart. It physically ached when she got near him. Sadly, the same held true when they were apart. She couldn't win.

"Let me out!" Liv hit the door. Her swollen hands throbbed, and her feet felt like they'd been turned into pulp. But what else could she do? Sit and wait? With luck, one of the men would get fed up and open the damned door. Then she'd greet him with a chair over the head.

Good luck with that, Liv. You'll need more than a chair to take one of those colossal beasts down.

The sad part was someone had already come for the day, leaving fruit and a sandwich while she'd been asleep like they'd done on two other occasions. They somehow knew the moment she was in the small attached bathroom or when she dozed off. A hidden camera or secret merman spy abilities? She didn't know, but this time she'd be ready. No more sleeping.

Just then, someone shoved a pink sheet of paper underneath the door. Liv picked it up and began to read, feeling like the wind had been knocked out of her. "Are these assholes serious?" she whispered, nibbling her fingernail.

Dear Landlover,

In preparation for your arrival to the sacred island of El Corazón, we'd like to remind you of a few simple rules to make your time more pleasant as well as keep you alive:

1. *The island is secret and you must never discuss it or its inhabitants with anyone. If you break this rule, we will know, and the punishment will be swift for not only you, but for those you hold dear.*
2. *We do not recommend going outdoors unescorted at night. If for some reason you*

must venture out during non-daylight hours, please stay clear of the beaches.

3. *Under NO circumstances are you permitted to swim in the ocean at night. Our waters are filled with deadly creatures who will devour you in seconds.*
4. *Should you come across one of our deadly creatures, we recommend you run; however, they are not to be harmed. Doing so is punishable by death, as they are sacred.*
5. *As you are a guest on this island for the sole purpose of participating in our time-honored Claiming Ceremony, we wish to highlight the following points:*
   a. *Your participation must be voluntary.*
   b. *After being claimed by one of our fine male specimens, you will be taken back to his quarters and bitten. This may cause some discomfort; however, we hope the remaining evening's activities, involving vigorous and pleasurable sexual intercourse, will detract from any pain.*
   c. *Immediately following your evening, if you notice a discoloration in the form of black spots on your skin, congratulations! You have been mated to one of our fine mermen and have been given the honor of becoming one of our sacred Maids. Note: our healer will attend to you during your transformation and see you safely to the ocean.*

d. *If you do not experience this discoloration, congratulations are still in order, as you have been chosen to carry one of our future mermen. Note: your merman will explain the rules pertaining to the child's care during its time with you as well as child support disbursement schedules.*
e. *If you have been claimed by a merman who is currently mated, we are sorry to inform you that you are ineligible to become a sacred Maid. (Refer to 5d.)*

6. *All landlover guests, except those who've been chosen to be Maids, are required to leave the island the morning immediately following your evening of claiming, as landlovers are hazardous to the delicately balanced ecosystem of the island.*

Any violation of the island's laws are punishable by death. We hope you enjoy your stay.

Sincerely,
El Corazón Island (as transcribed by the Elders)

Liv stared at the letter in complete horror and disbelief. The casual tone was comical and glib, while the words were frightening. Why would any woman in her right mind go for this?

Because they're not in their right minds. Everything about the island was pure and utter insanity, bordering on the edge of surreal and farcical. *I have to get Dana out of here.*

Liv returned to pounding the door. “Hey!” she screamed. “Can you crazy fucking bastards hear me? I know you can! You’re mermen. You hear everything! Open this fucking door!”

“Liv?” said a soft familiar voice on the other side of the door.

Ohmygod. “Dana? Honey? Open the door. You have to let me out.”

“Liv, the other ladies asked me to tell you to stop yelling. You’re totally ruining the last night of our party.”

Party? Fucking party? And they were almost to the island?

Liv placed her palms and forehead against the door. “Dana, I need you to listen to me. This isn’t a party. You are in danger. These people are not what you think.”

“Liv, I know everything. They already told us what they are. They even handed out these pamphlets that explain—”

“Dana! They’re mermen!” *Dammit.* Saying the word “mermen” made her feel crazy, too.

“Yes, Liv,” Dana said like an obstinate sixteen-year-old. Only, the real Dana was twenty-four and acted like it. She had a boyfriend and a great job working at the elementary school in Wrangell, Alaska, their hometown. “And I consider it an honor to have been chosen.”

They’ve brainwashed her.

"Dana, no." Liv's eyes filled with tears. "It's not an honor. It's horrible. You'll either end up pregnant or become some sort of animal." It was the most backwards and cruel thing she'd ever heard of. "They're barbaric assholes, Dana. And you don't want to get mixed up with them."

"They're not barbaric. They're beautiful, and I'd give anything for a night with one of them."

It sounded like the Stepford version of Dana speaking. They'd really messed with her head. "No! Don't listen, Dana. You don't want this. Think of Steve. You love Steve." Steve was Dana's live-in boyfriend. They'd been together since high school, and the two were planning to get married in a few years.

"I dumped Steve right before Mom and Dad's anniversary party."

"*What?* Why?" Liv found that very suspicious.

"I was tired of him always being such a wuss—look, Liv, I gotta go. That really hot one, Shane, said he wants to hang with me tonight, and I'm hoping he'll claim me tomorrow. So try to keep it down, okay?"

"Dana! Open this fucking door!"

There was no reply, and Liv sank to the floor, sobbing. *This isn't happening. This isn't happening.* These animals were going to ruin Dana's life. *Stop it, Liv. Stop wasting precious time crying over what should be.* Liv wiped the tears from her eyes and got up from the floor. Dana was counting on her. Not to mention their family, too. They had to be going insane with worry right now.

Okay. What are my options? Of course, there were only two: give Shane—an evil, untrustworthy bastard—what he wanted and pray he'd let Dana go like he promised. Or tell Shane to screw himself.

There has to be another choice. Think, Liv. Think.

She sat on her narrow bed with her eyes closed and focused on her breathing. *Okay. I know what to do.* The moment that door opened after they reached the island, she'd run for it and find Roen. She'd tell him everything and hope to God he'd get her out of this.

So what if Roen didn't help her, like in that dream? The last time she'd seen him, he made it clear he never wanted to see her again, and it had broken her heart. Then, within the space of a heartbeat, he'd changed into this angry, cruel version of himself and raised his hand to her. She still wasn't one hundred percent sure what had happened, because she'd seen how the island had begun to change him into something that frightened her. *One of them.*

Then there were those *other* urges of his. The ones that made him want to bite her and take her like an animal.

What if the civilized Roen doesn't exist anymore? Roen wouldn't be saving her. He'd be doing the opposite. *He's still your best option.* She only hoped there was some of the old Roen still left inside.

CHAPTER FOUR

Seven o'clock the next evening, the lack of motion woke Liv in the armchair with a prickly startle. *Oh crap.* Liv froze. *We're here.* She already felt the sick ominous energy of the island seeping through the walls. Ironically, the location itself was breathtaking—black and gold-sanded shores and a snowcapped peak surrounded by pine tree forest on all sides. Of course, that was camouflage.

Liv pressed her ear to the door and heard footsteps going up and down the passageway. They had to be unloading.

Okay. They'll be coming for you soon. Be ready. Stay calm.

Liv then noticed another sandwich had been left on the nightstand along with a change of clothes—a purple tank top and khaki shorts, no doubt borrowed from one of the other women onboard. They'd included a pair of black leather sandals.

Good. She'd need something to protect her feet when she ran through the rough terrain.

Liv quickly ate to keep up her strength, changed, and then sat herself calmly on the bed. *This is going to work. This is going to work. Just keep calm and make nice until you get outside.* She had to do everything possible to avoid getting tied up or shoved into a cage.

"Knock, knock!" a deep voice called from the other side of the door. "It's Jason. Remember me?"

How could she forget? He was one of Shane's "buddies" she'd met her first day on the island.

"Come in." She remained seated, not wanting to seem overly eager or show her hand.

"Are you going to attack me?" he asked.

"Not planning to, although the day is still young."

Jason popped open the door and peeked his head through, flashing his bright white, charming smile. His deeply tanned skin was the same as the last time they'd seen each other, only now he'd cut off his dreaded blond locks into a short, deceivingly civilized hairdo. "Good. Because I have one hell of a fucking hangover."

Liv refrained from showing how much that bothered her. He'd likely been partying with Dana and the other "guests."

"Nice look," she said. "Trying to impress the ladies?"

Jason ran his hand over his newly cropped hair. "Most of us aren't big on using brushes, so it's easier to cut it when we go to the mainland. But yeah, we try to tone down the scary factor for the ladies. Makes the process of getting their guard down much easier. Well, that and margaritas."

Liv resisted balling her fists and taking a swing. His cavalier attitude about this whole thing disgusted her.

"Well, I'm ready to go," she said, standing up from the bed.

Jason stepped all the way inside the room, wearing the traditional island garb of a simple piece of black cloth that hit mid-thigh and wrapped around the waist. No shoes, no shirts or coats—despite the somewhat chilly weather—just a little man skirt. The only thing Liv never understood was why some men wore black or red and Roen wore suede. Were they like kilts and each clan had a color?

"Not so fast, landlover. You sit." He pointed to the bed.

Oh no. Why? Liv's eyes focused on the open door behind him. There was no way in hell she'd get around this huge man and make it out.

"Are you going to hurt me?" she asked, looking to gauge his reaction.

He scoffed. "What? Me? Only if you run, in which case I'd kill you because those are my orders—not because I enjoy that sort of shit. But I know you'd never put me in that position because I can move ten times faster and have excellent night vision."

Oh crap. Change of plans. Perhaps she could sneak away before the Claiming Ceremony.

"Now sit." Jason pointed to the bed again.

Playing the role of obedient landlover, she placed a pleasant smile on her face, sat, and folded her hands neatly in her lap. "Okay. I'm sitting."

Jason closed the door, leaned against it, and stared at her with an awkward expression.

"Uh. What are we doing?" she asked.

"Waiting." He smiled.

Why is he looking at me like that? "For what?"

"For the signal Dana is off the ship. Shane's orders. He didn't want you upsetting her again."

Yeah, sure. Because Shane really cared about "upsetting" people. The more likely explanation was that Shane didn't want her to see where they took Dana.

"Okay," Liv said sedately. "Then we wait." Liv felt like a shaken soda can, ready to pop. *Dammit. Why is he still looking at me like that?* It wasn't helping her stay calm.

"So." Jason bobbed his head.

She bobbed her head back. "Yeah. So."

"This is weird, huh? You. Back here."

Was he on something? Or was this how mermen made small talk?

"Yep. So weird," she said flippantly. She looked at the floor, the ceiling, anywhere except Jason's face.

Finally, after several more awkward moments of silence, she couldn't take it anymore. "Okay. Why are you staring at me like that?"

Jason shrugged. "I'm trying to figure it out."

"What?"

"Why you asked Shane to bring you back after Roen discarded you. I mean, the shame alone would've kept me from ever showing my face here again. Yet here you are."

What? So Shane told everyone she wanted to be there, and they believed him? Had no one heard her screams over the last three days? And exactly what had Roen told everyone about her original departure? "What do you mean by discarded?"

"Liv, it's no secret Roen publically denounced you as his mate."

"It's a secret to me. Care to elaborate?" The more she knew about what she'd be going into, the better.

"He said you were far too weak and unintelligent even for reproduction."

What the hell? However, despite the sting of hearing she'd been publically declared "not good enough" for Roen, Liv had to put a rational spin on all this. Roen had made a huge sacrifice to free her after he'd fought and "won" her along with control over the island. But because he'd never completed the claiming ritual—he'd bitten her, but they never had sex—she knew Roen had to tell his men something.

"Personally," Jason continued studying her, "I don't think you look weaker than the other women—I mean, they're all weak—they're women, right? Regardless, I see how your lack of intelligence is a turnoff. On the other hand, I find that to be true of most human females, too."

My IQ could run laps around yours, blondie, she growled in her head.

He went on, "And, truthfully, we only need you for your wombs and mothering abilities, since none of your genes are carried on with our children."

"They're not?" the anthropologist in her couldn't help asking.

"Of course not. Otherwise, our species would be diluted with human blood, which is why only our men pass along DNA, and we only have male offspring. Anyway, if our leader says he could never risk having such a weak and feebleminded female to care for his progeny, who am I to argue?"

All right. Don't get angry. Remember, you don't want to be a part of this. She'd only wanted Roen. She still did, and that was something she desperately needed to get past. *It'll take time, that's all.*

On the academic side, however, Liv found this tidbit of reproductive info fascinating.

"Well," she stood up, "thank you for your honesty and words of encouragement to little old human female me."

"Sure. Anytime, Liv." He reached out and gave her shoulder a soft squeeze. "I know it's not your fault you're defective."

What a charmer. Jason literally had no filter, though she found that to be true of all the mermen she'd interacted with. They all spoke the language of Brutal Honesty.

"Don't you mean discarded?" she said condescendingly.

"No. You're immune to our charms. That definitely makes you defective."

Now Liv was rejected and defective? Wow. Any more flattery and she might have to change her identity to avoid the public shame. In all seriousness, though, she had no clue why their "charms" didn't work on her. A complete mystery. Just like the fact their sacred water, which could heal a dying man with a few drops, only sort of worked on her. She needed a gallon of that stuff to make minor healing happen. It was all very intriguing, though none of it actually mattered. Dana did.

"Welp. That's me. Feeble, weak, rejected, and defective," she said glibly.

"Hey, at least Shane wants you. That's a consolation."

No, not even a little. But his statement opened the door to the one really important question on the table: What was Shane up to? Shane hadn't fought for her during her first trip to "paradise for the insane." He'd said that she wasn't worth dying for. Not that she cared what he thought. It was simply a point. Shane had really gone out of his way to get her back. Why?

"Yes. Lucky, lucky me," she said, "especially considering my shortcomings. So why exactly do you think that is?"

"He belongs to the 'finders keepers' school of thought." Jason referred to the fact that Shane had spotted her drifting on the ocean after that fishing boat had gone down. "And our kind is known for being extremely possessive. Especially if the object happens to be a beautiful woman."

"So now Shane thinks I'm his mate?"

"He's already mated. He only wants to claim you for mindless sex and reproduction."

The thought of sex with that mer-madman made her nauseous. Although the truth was, thinking of sex with any man but Roen made her feel the same. The Shane factor merely raised the aversion level to extra-special-revolting.

"Besides," Jason continued, "if you were Shane's mate, you'd probably sense it and he'd be busy trying to keep everyone away until he claimed you. After that, he'd kill anyone who got between you or go crazy trying."

"Crazy?"

"Separating mates once they've found each other drives them mad. It's like depriving a person of air or food. They can't survive for very long."

"Wait." She folded her arms. "You're telling me that they literally go insane—straightjacket, padded-room insane?"

He scoffed. "Don't sound so shocked. We have hearts, you know. And there's nothing more important to a merman than his woman."

Liv felt a few random pieces click into place. Her feelings for Roen, from the first moment they'd met, had defied all logic. It was like a fire in her heart and soul she couldn't put out. Then, after leaving Roen behind on the island, she'd tried to move on with her life, only to find Roen infiltrated her dreams—when she managed to sleep—and occupied a solid portion of her daytime thoughts. The harder she'd pushed herself to think of something else, the more she burned to physically be near him. It was completely irrational. It had been driving her mad. However, if this mate thing was real, it explained everything. It explained why Roen had repeatedly laid his life on the line for her, too.

Oh God. I'm his mate. The realization startled her. Partially because she didn't know such a thing really existed. Yeah, she'd heard Roen mention the word, but she figured it was merman-lingo for a woman they considered to be "keepers" versus sex toys, or something like that. She'd had no idea what it really meant.

So did Roen know all this? If yes, why hadn't he told her?

"Jason, you said Roen denounced me. But if the connection between mates is so strong, how's that possible?"

"Obviously, you weren't his true mate. It's rare that we'd ever make that sort of mistake because it's not a choice—it's something that just happens. But I guess it's possible. Case in point, Roen refused to finish the claiming ritual with you and then had you tossed off the island. A merman would never be able to do that to his true mate. He wouldn't be able to resist her, and he'd definitely never separate from her voluntarily."

Liv felt more little clicks inside her head, the seemingly random pieces latching together and painting a bigger picture. Roen was the most stubborn, fearless, determined person she'd ever met. If anyone could defy the rules, he could. That meant he'd resisted his urge to be with her and then lied to his men. All probably in an effort to protect her somehow.

Except, maybe Shane didn't fall for it.

Liv's brain tingled—she knew she was onto something. *Ohmygod. Maybe none of this is really about me.* Otherwise, Shane would've gone for her the first time around. *Maybe Shane wants to pick a fight with Roen, using me as bait.* Why? What did Roen have that Shane wanted? The only answer she came up with was control of the island.

"Jason, what would happen if someone challenged Roen for the island?"

"Like who?"

"Does it matter?"

"Not really. Under our laws, anyone can challenge, although no one would be stupid enough to do it without a thumbs-up from the Big Girl herself. Why? Think you'll go for it?" He laughed.

Not in a million years. She wanted nothing to do with this place. Nevertheless, his discriminatory, backward attitude irritated her. "Maybe I will."

Jason shot her a look. "Women are only good for two things: being mermaids or making babies."

Liv sneered with revulsion. "Golly gee, Jason. Thank garsh we have you big strong men in little skirts to put us small-brained females in our places, garsh." She made a little hoedown rocking motion with her fist.

"You're welcome." He took a bow right when someone knocked on the door.

"About fucking time!" Jason yelled. "Next time, you babysit the crazy-stupid human."

This guy is such an ass!

"Okay, landlover." Jason yanked open the door. "Time to get you ready for tonight's big event."

Liv's stomach lurched. If she was right, then the situation was no longer about her and Dana, it was much bigger: Shane was planning a coup. And if Roen lost power, Shane might kill him and then do whatever he wanted with her and her sister.

The only problem now was she wasn't sure what to do. Running to Roen might be exactly what Shane wanted.

CHAPTER FIVE

Trying to keep her head out of the meltdown zone, Liv followed Jason into the dimly lit, narrow corridor lined with cabin doors, up several flights of carpeted staircases, and out onto the deck. Once her eyes adjusted a little to the darkness, more of the ship came into focus, including the hot tub, lounge chairs, shuffleboard, and bar. The place was a regular Carnival Cruise ship. *With scary mermen.*

Her eyes then spotted an even larger yacht moored at the pier. Dozens of boats filled the massive harbor.

"Holy crap," she half gasped. She really couldn't believe all this was here. The first time she'd come, none of it had been visible. Just one big island with a giant peak in the middle and a few cabins sprinkled around the forest.

Jason smiled at her. "The big boat's Roen's."

She almost wanted to laugh. Of course it was. That man didn't believe in small.

"Where is everyone?" she asked, noticing the empty ship. More importantly, where was Dana?

"Our guests are in their bungalows, getting ready." He pointed to the forested hillside overlooking the marina, glowing with lots of lights. "And, of course, the ladies are in their usual spot, so don't get too close." Jason pointed to the water. "Hi, ladies!" he said cheerfully.

Liv looked down into the black water, where thousands of big yellow eyes bobbed in the gentle waves. "Holy shit!" She instinctively jumped toward Jason. Of course, the moment she realized it, she stepped away. But not too far away.

"Don't worry," he said, "they're forbidden from going on the piers or land during the Collection. Otherwise, they'd eat all the guests. But don't get any ideas about going out for a midnight sail; they'd eat you faster than you could say 'hungry, hungry mermaid.'"

Liv nodded absentmindedly, staring at the flickering orbs. As frightening as the creatures were, her heart went out to them.

"So do they know what's happening?" Liv asked.

"Of course. They're mermaids, not mindless fish—hell, most of the newer ones have college degrees."

Oh God. They were women like her, trapped inside those bodies. *Except they eat anything that moves.*

Liv carefully disembarked the ship, staying in the center of the gangway and dock, closely following Jason. *If they make a move, I'm throwing him in the water.* Those sharp teeth were literally four feet away, lurking between the boat slips.

Jason and Liv then made their way out of the marina up a windy dirt path toward several clusters of cottages. She still couldn't believe all this. The place looked like a five-star luxury island retreat.

"Is that how this all works?" she asked, slightly winded from the climb. "You comb the beaches for women and tell them they're going to some exclusive resort?"

"No. We do *not* comb beaches. We have standards. And we have scouts with very good instincts who go out and do a little preselection. Here we are." He stopped in front of a brown cottage with white shutters, nestled between two colossal pine trees that soared toward a star-filled sky. Potted flowers, with little lights around the edges, illuminated the flagstone walkway to the front door.

"I'll wait outside while you get ready," Jason said. "You'll find the ceremonial dress and white sandals you're to wear in the bedroom closet. There are snacks and beverages in the kitchen. I suggest the champagne—it's a favorite with the ladies."

Liv glanced at Jason skeptically.

"I meant the human ladies," he added. "Mermaids don't drink. Not alcohol, anyway. Blood is another story altogether."

Liv made a sour face—"Thanks"—and walked toward the front door.

"The back door is bolted," Jason called out, "so don't try sneaking off."

Of course it was.

"Oh!" he added. "And Shane asked me to remind you that you're not to go looking for Dana. He said he doesn't want her upset again."

Reaching for the door, Liv gritted her teeth. What Shane meant was that he would get upset and hurt Dana. *Bastard.*

Liv entered the dark cottage and slammed the door shut before leaning against it. What the hell was she going to do? Shane had her backed into a corner. A big scary, cobweb-filled corner with giant fanged spiders and boogie men.

Running to Roen was no longer a smart move. What if that was what Shane wanted—to start some big fight? Going along with Shane's demands and pretending she wanted him would also provoke an ugly confrontation because, like Jason said, nobody got between a merman and his mate.

Goddammit. Goddammit! All of these options led to very heinous places.

What if I prevent Roen from fighting for me at all? What if she convinced Roen that she didn't want him anymore? After all, she was "defective," so maybe she could convince him that her mate feelings had gone away.

No, it wasn't a permanent solution, in terms of Shane going after Roen, though it would buy her time to figure out what to do next and keep Dana from being claimed.

Of course, if she was successful, she might actually end up becoming Shane's for the night.

Liv's entire soul bucked in protest, but there simply wasn't another option. Liv ran her hand over the wall next to the door and found the light switch.

"Hello, Liv."

"Fuck!" Liv jumped.

With his hands casually in his pockets, Roen stood at the other end of the cozy living room—decorated in a nautical theme with powder-blue walls, paintings of sailboats, and large seashells on the distressed white coffee table. Like the last time she'd seen him, both in person and in her dream, Roen wore a crisp white dress shirt and dark, well-tailored pants that accentuated every inch of his tall, masculine form.

"Nice to see you, too," he said in that slow, arrogant, deep voice before casually strolling toward a small table in the corner topped with a tray of clean glasses and several liquor bottles. He poured a tall glass of something, scotch perhaps, threw it back, and then stared with flaring nostrils, his thick arms over his broad chest. All the while, Liv watched his every move, trying to keep herself calm. She knew his laid-back stance was for show, because a look of pure rage flickered in his hypnotic green eyes.

"Roen, what are you doing here?"

"You sound afraid."

Of course. She had no clue if Roen was a threat. The man had changed. Bigger. Meaner. Deadlier.

Then there was her. Five seven, medium build, about as much muscle as a mussel.

"I'm not afraid," she lied. "I just know how you can get." She discreetly placed her hand on the door handle at her back, ready to run.

"You may remove your hand from the door. I'm much more controlled these days," he said, his voice low and menacing. "When I want to be."

So much for discreet. She'd forgotten how mermen had better hearing along with the eyesight.

"So…why are you here?" She dropped her hands, attempting to appear calm and indifferent; meanwhile her eyes wouldn't stop moving up and down, gliding over his beautiful body, drinking in every inch of him. His shape, right down to the wide width of his shoulders and narrow waist, was pure seduction material. Not too beefy and bulky, but tall, solid, and sublimely male. And his face, though now sporting a short rich-brown beard, was nothing shy of breathtaking, including those sensual lips that balanced between silky soft and firm, just perfect for wrapping around a throbbing nipple. *Or lower.*

As if reading her suggestive thoughts, his intensely carnal gaze moved down, down, down and lingered over the body part longing for his attention.

Don't, Liv. Don't show him what he does to you.

She cleared her scratchy throat. "Why. Are. You. Here?"

His sinfully seductive gaze crawled up her body, leaving every inch of her skin tingling. "Why am I here? I live here, which you already know. So I believe I should be directing that question to you."

"The reason is no one's business but my own."

"Bullshit. Who's the stupid asshole that came to collect you?" His body didn't move, but his eyes told her he was holding back a tornado of caustic rage.

Liv's panic button began flashing bright red. "Roen—"

"Tell me, goddammit. Who. Is. The *foking* asshole. That brought you back to the island?"

Make him believe, Liv. Do what you have to do to make him believe.

"I'm not sure that matters since I want to be here. I even brought my sister."

"I won't tolerate you lying to me, Liv."

She shrugged. "Why would I lie? Even you have to admit that merman charms are pretty impressive."

He looked away, grinding his jaw, and ran his strong hand through his silky, jaw-length hair. "Those charms don't work on you," he replied so sharply, the words nearly cut through her charade. He knew her too well. She had to convince him she came for some other reason.

"Doesn't matter. I'm still a woman and what woman wouldn't want to be fucked by one of the beautiful men on this island. Personally, I'm hoping to land Shane."

Roen's eyes narrowed on her face, and his chest expanded with rapid breaths. "Shane? You expect me to believe that?"

"It doesn't matter what you think or expect, Roen," she said, doing her best impression of a heartless bitch. "You made it perfectly clear you didn't want me." She wagged her finger at him. "And shame, shame on you," she purred, "because I was left with a craving I can't seem to satisfy with just any man. And trust me, I've tried. Boy, oh boy, how I've tried. With dozens and dozens of men," she lied. "However, I'm betting that my needs *can* be satisfied by a merman—any merman—since you all have exceptional equipment."

Roen stormed across the room and stared down at her with cold, calculating eyes, causing Liv to push her body firmly against the door. "I'm not buying the act, Liv. And I have to believe that somewhere deep down inside you know my rejection was to protect you."

"Pah!" She barked out a little laugh. "Roen, dear, haven't you figured out by now that I used you to save myself? I did it again when we saw each other in Seattle. Your little bitch of an island wanted to come after me because I broke my promise not to tell. And once again, there was big strong Roen ready to come to my rescue." She laced her fingers together and rested her chin on the backs of her hands, batting her eyelashes. "Oh, save me, Roen. Save me!" She dropped her hands and laughed. "Like I said when we first met: you're an ass. You'll always be an ass, and now it's time for you to leave. I need to get ready. For. Shane," she added.

A cold glaze of hostility washed over Roen's face. Even the color of his green eyes seemed to darken a bit. She had no idea if she'd convinced him, but she was sure as hell she'd wounded him. Would it be enough?

Roen began unbuttoning his shirt while keeping his hard, angry eyes pinned to her face.

"Wha-what are you doing?" she asked.

"What does it look like?" He shed his shirt and threw it to the floor.

Oh no. Is he calling my bluff? Because no way could Liv hide her true emotions if he started kissing her or touching her or showing her his perfectly chiseled pectoral muscles and hard rippling abs that ended with those teasing little grooves that cut diagonally over his hip bones.

She drew an unsteady breath.

He then unbuttoned his pants and slowly unzipped, making a seductive show of it. All the while, Liv felt her body igniting into an erotic blaze. She didn't need to see him naked to know what was under that zipper. She'd memorized every inch of his superbly portioned, long, thick penis. Oh yes, it held an especially sinful place in the back of her mind, with its very own shelf. Sadly, they'd never had sex, but she'd felt the tip of him push against her entrance, and since that moment, she'd longed for the rest.

Roen shed his pants—*Oh, God. He's commando*—and kicked them aside. Liv held her breath, willing her gaze to remain stuck to his eyes.

Don't look. Don't look. He'll know how much you want him.

"Trying to impress me?" she said with an affected little smirk. "Because I assure you Shane's gear is twice as nice."

His right eye twitched, and then the corner of his sensual lips curled into a wickedly arrogant smirk. "Doubtful." He stepped in closer, leaving only a few inches between them. The air began to buzz with that strange energy he produced when aroused. And there was no denying the heat filling the narrow space separating their bodies, especially the spot where Roen's now naked erection gently pushed against her stomach.

He's not playing fair.

Liv fought the need to lick her lips and press them to his mouth or kneel down and taste him on her tongue—something she'd also never gotten the opportunity to do and had fantasized about on more than one occasion.

"Well," she said with a shaky voice and gulped, "whatever it is you think you're doing won't work. I'm here for claiming, and you're not who I w-w-want to spend the night with."

"Excellent. Can you hand me that? I just flew in, so I didn't have time to change." His eyes momentarily flashed to a small side table next to the front door.

She followed his gaze and noticed a piece of folded suede. She grabbed the thing and quickly pushed it to his bare chest. "Here you go." She then swallowed the prickly lust-filled lump in her throat.

You are not affected. You do not want to touch him. You do not want to wrap your fingers around his cock and pleasure the seed right out of him. Oh yes, she did. She'd watched him come once, and it was hands down the most erotic thing she'd ever witnessed. Right now, she felt her panties steaming up just thinking about it.

"Thanks." He slid the suede from her hand, making a point to make contact with her fingers. The sensation sent a spear of throbbing warmth right between her legs, almost like he'd touched her intimately with those hot, thick fingers.

Still holding his gaze tightly to her face, he wrapped the cloth around his waist. "Excuse me."

Liv blinked. "Sorry?"

"I have to go now; the ceremony is starting soon. If you'll excuse me."

She was blocking the door. "Oh. Sorry." She stepped aside and looked at her feet—the only safe place.

"Enjoy your night with Shane, Liv. I hope he makes all of your fantasies come true."

"He's a merman. I'm sure he will." Her voice came out raspy and quivering.

Roen left and she shut the door behind her.

"Fuck, fuck, fuck," she whispered, pressing her back to the door. That had been the most difficult thing she'd ever had to do. Not the lying part, but the resisting him part. Her entire body screamed for that man, especially the parts that were now wet, hot, and needed release. None of that compared, however, to how badly her heart ached for him.

God, I hope I convinced him. There was less than an hour before the Claiming Ceremony, and then she'd have to convince him once again.

Chapter Six

Keeping his emotions hidden, Roen gave a cool nod to the man standing guard outside Liv's cottage when he passed. Inside Roen's mind, a violent storm raged, and he knew exactly who was to blame: *Fucking Shane.*

Did Liv honestly think he would ever believe she wanted that man or any other, for that matter? He could smell the lust on Liv's skin and the scent of her arousal between her legs from the moment they locked eyes. It took every ounce of restraint not to act on his own urges, but when he picked up the hint of fear in Liv's dark eyes, he knew she was protecting someone she loved. Was it her sister or him?

Perhaps both.

The thought of her loving him sped up his heart. Yes, mates wanted with every fiber of their being, although the want was a force of nature. The wind blew, you were a sail, and away you'd go. However, love was not a given between mates.

It doesn't matter if she loves you. It was inevitable that he'd only destroy Liv like his father had destroyed his mother. *Or perhaps Liv'll end up a maid.* No, he and Liv would never be together because he refused to hurt her.

However, that meant he needed to do everything possible to free Liv's heart from the bond between them. It had never been done that he knew of, not that it *foking* mattered. He would find a way. He would save her from the fate of being a merman's mate.

First things first: Get her the hell away from here.

Roen knew exactly why Shane brought Liv's sister to the island—leverage against Liv. But why bring Liv at all?

Roen headed straight to Naylor's cottage. The old man was one of their five elders and knew more about their laws and history than anyone else. He was also a stubborn, cantankerous old goat.

Roen knocked on the door of the rustic, pine cabin and entered without bothering to wait for permission. After all, Roen was king here. That, and Naylor was in some other world half the time.

"Well, do come in," said Naylor sarcastically. As usual, the old man sat with his eyes closed in his worn leather reading chair positioned an arm's length from a wall of ancient texts. His long white hair and beard covered his bare, upper torso like a warm blanket.

"Good. You're awake. Why did Shane bring Liv back?" Roen asked.

Naylor opened one green eye and then the other. "You really have to ask?"

Roen shot him a look. "I'm standing here asking, so I think that answers your question."

"He obviously wants control of the island."

"You told me only Dorans are chosen by the island to rule," Roen argued.

"That doesn't mean a non-Doran can't. It means it's never happened. And I will tell you that Shane's family has tried over many generations."

"And the island will allow it?" Roen asked.

Naylor flicked his bony wrist. "The island is only as strong as the men who protect her, which is why she wants only the smartest, fiercest warrior leading. If it happens to be someone else, I doubt she'll care."

"Then why not challenge me for leadership? Why bring landlovers into this?"

"You mean the woman Liv?" Naylor scowled when he said her name. "The one you say isn't your mate because she's not strong enough, yet she was chosen by this island to come here, and then managed to motivate you—the most stubborn sonofabitch on the planet—to step up and take over. You mean *that* landlover?"

"Yes. That landlover." What else could he say? The connection with the island made it hard to keep secrets. So if Naylor knew he'd lied about Liv, then others did, too, including Shane.

Naylor puckered his lips into a little ball and narrowed his green eyes in contemplation. "I do not know. Perhaps Shane hopes you'll never make it to a formal challenge. Mermen are known to lose their heads when it comes to their women."

Naylor might be right. Ungoverned killing and fighting among mermen was forbidden and punishable by death except under certain circumstances like self-defense. Disputes and challenges had to be settled in the great hall after each side declared their positions in a formal manner among witnesses. Otherwise, given their kind's short fuses and instincts for killing, their race would be extinct by now.

"I'm close to getting everyone what they want: freedom and their mates returned," Roen said. "Why would Shane want to risk losing that?" It was merely a question of time before Roen had the proper modern resources in place to keep anyone and everyone off the island.

"Not everyone wants change, Roen. Especially the island. It makes her nervous."

Well, too damned bad. Roen would do everything in his power to ensure she wasn't vulnerable to outsiders, but this chaos had to end. Besides, sooner or later, someone would discover this place. With technology and human population growth, the world grew smaller by the second. For God's sake, it was a damned miracle that an ocean freighter hadn't rammed right into them. Thousands of ships passed within two miles of their shores every damned year. Roen had no doubt in his mind that he'd get the island to come around. First, he needed to prove to her how his way would be better in the long run.

"And you?" Roen asked. "How do you feel about change?"

Naylor grinned. "No matter what you do, I will never leave her. She is my home. And may I remind you, Roen, that none of us will ever truly be free. She's as much a part of us as we are of her."

Being connected to something didn't mean it had to be everything. The connection simply needed to be honored and understood for what it truly was. What they had on this island wasn't right.

And I'm going to change that. And Shane just made a big mistake dragging my mate into this.

The sound of a loud metal bell rang out across the island, summoning everyone for the evening's big event. It was time.

With a heavy sigh, Naylor watched Roen disappear out the front door. He admired the young man of only thirty-four years for his determination and loyalty to the people. Nevertheless, this island was no place for a merman with a big heart. Because despite the island's name—El Corazón—she didn't possess a heart. It was the one thing Naylor understood after living here for hundreds of years: the island always got what the island wanted.

One way or another. Those who moved against her wishes got to see everything they loved taken away, piece by piece. *Never turn your back on that which the island asks of you.* It was the cardinal rule.

"Why did you remain silent, merman?" the island hissed inside Naylor's head. *"Why did you not tell him?"*

"Because Roen was in no mood to listen and telling him now would only fuel his conviction."

"Then let him fuel himself to the grave and everyone who chooses to follow him," she said. *"Roen made a vow to rule obediently if I spared his mate. He promised to close his heart to her and give it to me."*

It had been a mistake—her mistake—calling Roen to the island, using his mate as the carrot to get him to dethrone his own brother. But the island couldn't help herself. She had believed Roen's strength would make her stronger, too. However, she quickly realized there was such a thing as too strong. She couldn't control him like she'd been able to with the others. That hadn't kept her from trying, though, and tonight would be her last attempt to rein him in. Roen either buckled or Shane would step in. Liv was merely brought in as a test for Roen, a bone to fight over.

"There is still a chance Roen'll keep his word. And we both know how happy that would make you."

"Yes, but if Roen so much as lifts a finger toward that landlover bitch, I will make him watch while I kill everything he loves—his mate, his brother, the men, and perhaps I'll take out some of those vile landlovers, too."

This was what Naylor had been afraid of. The island's sense of justice and revenge was one without regard for the consequences. Sometimes protecting her meant protecting her from herself, too. "I will personally see to it that the landlover female is dealt with. But please, my queen, I beg you to let the men live."

"No one, except for the elders and Shane, will be spared if Roen fails to keep his vow. And there will be no limit to the suffering I will bring."

"But my queen—"

"No! Weakness and disobedience are like a cancer that must be eradicated before it spreads. I will tolerate none of it. Do you hear me, merman?"

Naylor nodded and wrung his tired hands. "Understood, my queen." In the meantime, he would gather the other elders and begin discussing how to keep their people from being wiped from existence.

CHAPTER SEVEN

"Wait. Where are you taking me?" Liv stopped cold on the narrow dark path that cut through the pitch-black forest filled with thorny bushes. "This isn't the way to the great hall."

The great hall, where they'd taken her last time, was a giant cavern smack in the middle of the island, inside a mountain resembling a dormant volcano. Right now, it felt like they were heading in another direction.

Jason, who'd been taking the lead, stopped and turned. "That's because we're not going to the great hall. We're going to the lagoon."

"Why?" Frankly, Liv wasn't aware they even had a lagoon. Then again, this entire place was full of surprises. The bathroom in that cottage, for example, had a sauna and a double-headed shower with the most incredible water pressure ever, and she'd enjoyed every minute of it. *Forget last meals and last rites—a last shower is how this woman wants to go down.* She might not make it out of this Claiming Ceremony alive if things went south with Shane. Yes, it scared the hell out of her. So what? That wouldn't change a damned thing.

Jason chuckled, and Liv wished she could see his face. Had that been an evil villain chuckle?

"I get," she said, "that you guys have excellent night vision, but would it kill you to use a flashlight when 'guests' are around?" Her body already felt like a solid ball of nerves, and traipsing around in a dark chilly forest, getting stuck with thorns wasn't helping.

Jason chuckled once more.

"Why the hell are you laughing?" she grumbled.

"I find your spunk amusing, that's all. Sort of reminds me of a little piranha with sharp teeth—kinda cute."

Naturally, a merman would find a piranha cute.

"Come on," he said. "We're almost there, and you don't want to be late."

Oh no. Late. How tragic. She quickly imagined some horrible scene where women, with bite marks all over their bodies, writhed on the ground, screaming for mercy while they transformed into mermaids.

The dirt path sloped downward, and the front of Liv's sandal caught on a small rock. She stumbled and caught herself on the trunk of a sticky pine tree.

"Great." She pulled her sap-covered hands from the bark and wiped them down the sides of her white dress, which was really only a long strip of cloth wrapped around the body and tied behind the neck. It was what they'd made her wear the last time she'd been claimed when twenty men stepped up to fight to the death for her. Roen, of course, had decided to skip all that and challenge Lyle, his brother, for control of the island. Liv never got the story of how Lyle ended up in this place, though she knew it had to be complicated because up until that day, Roen believed his brother to be dead.

"Can you possibly walk any slower?" Jason chided.

"Yes. I can. And I don't want to hear a…" She looked up to address Jason, losing her train of thought. Through the stand of trees up ahead, she caught a glimpse of giant floodlights shining down on an enormous swimming hole.

She marched forward, passing Jason, for a better look. "Sonofabitch," she muttered under her breath, emerging from the forest onto a rocky ledge overlooking the pool of sparkling, deep green water. Four floodlights anchored to tall pine trees shined down on the water's surface. A fifth light illuminated a narrow, ten-foot-high waterfall. "You have a lake."

Jason stood beside her and shrugged. "Sure. Why wouldn't we? Doesn't everyone need drinking water?"

That wasn't the point. When she'd been shipwrecked on this island, before Roen took over, she'd been dying of thirst. Yes, dying-dying—not a figure of speech. Poor Roen, who'd showed up and rescued her from Shane's evil clutches, had to carry her in search of drinking water, but they'd never found any. Meanwhile, this damned lagoon had been ten minutes' walking distance from them the entire time. Of course, she and Roen hadn't been able to see it. *Thank you. I hope someone blows you up*, she thought to the island, who'd surely been responsible.

"It's not a lake," Jason said. "It's technically a lagoon with a waterfall. The water comes off the mountain when the snow melts." He pointed back toward the center of the island.

A loud sound filled the air, and that's when Liv spotted Roen standing at the top of the waterfall across the lagoon. He held a conch in his hand and blew into it like a horn. His stomach muscles flexed, showing off his ten-pack, and his bicep bulged with sleek hard muscle.

Don't look, Liv. Do not look at the hot merman wearing almost nothing.

"Crap. We're late." Jason grabbed her arm and pulled her down the trail that skirted the edge of the lagoon and led to a small beach, where the fifty other women waited, all wearing the same white dresses.

Still no Dana. Liv wasn't sure if she should be relieved or worried.

"Where's my sister?" she asked, stumbling behind Jason and his large strides.

"She's safe. Don't worry," he said curtly.

Why would I worry? she thought. *This place is like fucking Disneyland.*

Roen blew into his shell once again, and she forced herself to avert her gaze in order to keep her head clear—something impossible to do when she looked at that man. *Built for sinful, hard, hot sex, and I want to suck and lick and—*

"God." She winced. "Stop it."

Jason led her to the pack of women, who stared, drooled, and oh-ah'd in Roen's direction. "Wait. Isn't that Roen Doran?" one of the women murmured.

"Ohmygod. Yes. That's him," said another, squealing.

The women started buzzing excitedly. "I hope he claims me," said another. And then they all jumped in. "No, me. I want him." The voices turned into a flurry of lustful, X-rated commentary, and it took every ounce of willpower Liv possessed to fight the urge to tell them to keep their slutty eyes off her man.

"Liv." Jason gave her arm a squeeze. "The other women have been warned already. You have not. You are not to leave this beach under any circumstances until this event is over. If you must go to the bathroom, there's the spot." He pointed to the closest pine tree. "And if you break this rule, you will be fed to the maids. Do you understand?"

Liv nodded; meanwhile the women continued their happy, bachelorette-party banter. Roen was the main attraction.

"What is all this?" she asked.

"It is the Sinningitainnartok," Jason replied and yanked off the cloth around his waist.

Liv gasped and stepped back. "What the hell, Jason?" She tried not to look at his penis, but it was right there. Thick and long and pink and…well, dangling there between his muscled thighs, sprouting from a patch of coarse dark blond hair.

The women began screaming with delight. “Oh, yeah! Take it off, merman!”

Liv wanted to scream, too, but with frustration. This was a goddamned nightmare of one bizarre event after another, and these fifty women were so doped up on “merman” they seriously believed this was fun.

Jason flashed a dimpled smile and dipped his head. “Thank you, ladies. Thank you.”

Liv pushed his shoulder. “Jason, what the hell is this?” she demanded, and the women began booing her. Liv ignored them and instead stared angrily at Jason.

“It’s the Sinningitainnartok,” he said. “It’s a word meaning ‘awake all night.’ It’s also a formal ceremony where we—”

Roen’s deep, authoritative voice filled the air, cutting him off.

Everyone instantly silenced.

“I would like to thank our guests,” Roen said, looking down at the crowd of smiling, excited women from his spot high up on the waterfall’s ledge, “for joining us in this time-honored tradition. Tonight, the men will compete in a variety of challenges to determine who will participate in the Claiming Ceremony tomorrow evening. Per our ancient and sacred laws, only those who complete the challenges may claim a woman.”

The women applauded.

Did this mean if Shane didn't qualify, she'd be off the hook?

Liv started clapping, too. *Dear God, please don't let him pass.*

"Let the Sinningitainnartok begin." Roen whipped off his suede and dove into the water head first with an elegant swan dive, eliciting a wave of groupie-like screams in praise for his penis from the ladies.

Liv snarled.

"That's my cue," said Jason and dove into the lagoon. That's when Liv realized the rest of the men were already in the water, their heads popping up, taking deep breaths.

"Where'd they come from?" Liv asked, astonished.

A brunette with freckles on her nose and long bangs, standing to Liv's side, said, "Oh, they were just warming up for the big breath-holding challenge."

Treading water in the center of the lagoon, surrounded by his men, Roen called out, "The hour starts now."

An hour? Holy Christ.

One of the women, a redhead with short hair, standing toward the front, held up a stopwatch and gave it a click. "Go!"

Nice. Crowd participation, Liv thought.

The men disappeared into the depths of the lagoon, and Liv couldn't help but hold her breath, too.

The same woman to her side whispered, "I hear some of the men never come back up."

"What do you mean?" Liv asked.

The woman shrugged. "They told us all sorts of stories on the ship and one of them said that there are tunnels and currents down there. Some of the men get sucked in and never make it out."

"The island probably eats them," Liv mumbled.

"Ha!" The woman laughed. "Well, she'll have to get in line. Because we came a long way for a nibble of delicious merman."

Liv grimaced. "Yeah." She tried not to think about the sad, horrific truth of the situation or the fact she couldn't do anything to stop it. Of course, these women knew full well what was coming, and they couldn't be happier. It would take a miracle to stop this thing.

She then thought about Roen down there in the water. For some reason, she didn't feel worried—*That man is a survivor.*

As for Shane, she prayed she'd never see his face again.

After forty-five minutes, the first head surfaced and the man emerged from the water. His facial expression—shame—contrasted sharply with his rude exterior—long black hair in a braid down his back, a black beard, shimmering green eyes, and a tattoo of two crossing tridents over his chest.

The women applauded loudly, saying words of encouragement. "Awww, Zale, that's okay. We still love you."

The women sighed at his impressive manhood and then turned their attention toward his round solid ass as he disappeared into the forest.

"Well, ladies, most are still in the running," said Stopwatch Redhead.

Liv began nibbling her index finger. *Please no Shane. Please no Shane.*

A few more minutes passed and several more men surfaced—a blond guy with a fanged serpent tattoo that wrapped around his leg and lower abdomen, and another man with cropped brown hair who had biceps the size of cement bags. Each "loser" made the walk of shame out of the water while the women savored the opportunity to ogle every inch and make catcalls.

Finally, the hour was up. However, the men didn't resurface like she expected. "They don't have watches," she realized, meaning they'd stay down in the dark water for as long as they could and hope it was long enough.

Another half hour ticked by at an excruciatingly slow pace, and Liv found herself standing ankle deep in the water. Almost all of the men had come up for air—one hundred and eighty-nine, to be exact.

Still no Roen and no Shane.

Okay. Don't worry. I'm sure everything's fine, she told herself.

Another man appeared—Asian with a dreaded mohawk, scale tattoos on one arm, and Japanese symbols on the other—who looked like the world's tallest Samurai. *Not Roen.*

The beach, now crowded with a horde of wet naked men and flirty horny women, had turned into a little party. Someone had even broken out the champagne. From where? Who the hell knew?

"Shouldn't somebody go down there and get them?" And by "them," Liv meant Roen.

No one paid her any attention. The men were far too busy enjoying their fans' attention.

This is ridiculous. I'm going in. Liv waded deeper, readying to dive in, only to be pulled back.

"Uh-uh-uuuh," Jason warned. "No leaving the beach, Liv. Not until it's over—and even then, you're not to go off. There are more events."

"He could be stuck down there."

"Shane is our best swimmer. He'll be fine."

"Shane? Who the hell cares about…" Her voice faded. She needed to be pretending to want Shane, not Roen. "Oh, sorry. I thought you said Roen. And who the hell cares about that dirty bastard, right?"

Jason shrugged his golden brows. No, she wasn't sure what he'd meant by it, although her best guess landed on him thinking she might be full of shit.

Liv turned her attention back toward the surface of the water, nibbling away on her stump of a fingernail again.

Ten or so more heads came up—she'd lost count at this point.

Then a head of thick black hair floated up. *Shane. Fucking Shane.*

Triumphantly, he lifted his head from the water and howled. "Woo. Yay!" He swam toward Liv and then stood from the water, flashing a cocky grin. "Miss me, babe?"

She pasted on a disgusted smile—the best she could do at the moment. "Yeah. Congratulations." Her eyes went back to the middle of the lagoon.

Shane laughed sadistically. "Don't hold your breath, Liv. He's our worst swimmer. Could drown in a damned bathtub."

Liv's veins filled with hard, cold angst. She didn't know Roen was a bad swimmer.

"Come on." Shane grabbed her hand and pulled her toward him.

She snapped it away. "Don't touch me," she snarled.

"Remember our deal, Liv," he whispered, narrowing his wicked green eyes at her. "Remember who you really want."

Liv closed her eyes and got a hold of herself. Shane's point was well taken, and frankly, her actions weren't serving anyone.

Liv slowly sloshed her way from the water and headed toward the far end of the crowded beach, where she nonchalantly kept an eye on the surface. Another ten minutes ticked by, and Liv couldn't hold back the tears. Roen wasn't coming up. Why? He was their worst swimmer. He should've been up by now.

As calmly as possible, Liv walked over to Stopwatch Redhead, who stood talking to one of the tattooless "winners," an eight-foot-tall African American merman, with clear green eyes, a shaved head, and twelve-pack.

"Um, excuse me," Liv said politely, "how long has it been now?"

The woman held out the watch, unwilling to tear her eyes away from the perfect manly specimen before her.

Crap. One hour fifty minutes? Merman or not, Roen had been under the water for an impossible amount of time.

"Anyone know the record?" Liv called out.

"Hour and forty," one of the men replied.

I can't take this. Her fear for Roen wasn't something she could control. She loved him. So much it made her entire body ache and weep when she thought of anything happening to him.

She began to run for the water right when Roen's head abruptly emerged with a loud grunt-slash-gasp. Liv let out a sob of relief and then turned away to hide her face. She didn't want Roen to see what a wreck she was.

The crowd cheered for Roen having set a new record of sorts; meanwhile Liv's angry fists begged to be unleashed on Roen's face. *Damned sonofabitch is setting records while I'm falling apart thinking he's dead? I'll kill him!*

Liv took a moment to calm herself. She then wiped the tears from her eyes, glued a plastic-as-hell smile on her face, and turned toward the crowd, pretending to listen to some silly conversation about fishing barehanded. Through the many faces of insanely tall men towering over the adoring flock of five-foot-something females, those hypnotic green and hazel eyes caught her attention. Liv's smile melted away while his angry gaze burned right through her. It lasted only a moment, but Liv instantly knew that his little "record breaking" display had been a punishment meant for her. He'd wanted to cause her a little worry.

Or maybe it was a test, Liv. She put back her smile and turned it toward Shane.

The rest of the night, the men participated in one challenge after another—pushing down large pine trees, cracking boulders with one fist, harpooning fish from shore—each event was a display of skill and strength that Liv suspected was as much for the women's enjoyment as it was for narrowing down the pack of male participants in the Claiming Ceremony to come.

By the time the sun came up and the sky burst with electric blues, the Sinning-whatever-whatever-they-called-it finally came to a ceremonious close on the beach with seventy-five men left. Sadly, Shane was one of them, as was Roen. Liv tried not to think about what would happen next.

Would Roen choose a woman, too? She knew the island had demanded he have children when he'd negotiated for her freedom. *I hope to God I don't have to watch him fight for another woman.* It would break her damned heart. Add to that, she wasn't exactly free, now was she? It felt like an extra-special slap in the face.

Jason, who'd been eliminated toward the end, walked Liv back to her cottage. "See, that wasn't so bad, was it?" he said.

Liv felt too tired to talk. Keeping her eyes off of Roen the entire night had taken everything out of her. Anything she had left over went to not vomiting every time Shane touched her.

"Well," Jason said, "I always enjoy the Sinningitainnartok. Even if I already have a mate."

Liv slogged behind Jason up the dirt path leading past a large cluster of beautifully kept brown cottages next to hers. "If you've already found a mate, then why do you have to participate at all?"

"That's the difference between us and humans. Our heart and soul might belong to one woman, but everyone has to do their part when it comes to reproduction."

Liv already knew that their mates ended up monsters, so she guessed the lack of monogamy made sense from a species-survival aspect.

"Yep, gotta spread the love," he added and then gave his groin a little rub.

"Classy, Jason."

"Just tellin' it like it is, not that we expect you landlovers to understand. We just expect you to play ball. Or with our balls."

Har, har, she thought, but didn't respond.

They arrived at her cottage, and Liv caught a glimpse of Jason's tired face when she walked past him. There was a coldness in those bright green eyes she hadn't really noticed before.

She stopped and tilted her head, trying to figure him out.

"What?" he said defensively.

He's lying. Men didn't walk around with that sort of pain when they were "okay" with things.

"What would you give to get her back?"

Jason's snide little smile flattened into a straight line. "What do you mean?"

"Your mate. What would you give to get her back?" she asked, wanting to know if her suspicion was correct—he didn't really want to be doing these claimings.

"Everything. Which doesn't really matter, because she's not coming back."

"Roen might change things," she said.

Jason looked down at his bare feet. "Not likely. And if he did, she's gone. Her soul has left her body. The only way I'll ever see her again is in the afterlife."

"How do you know that?" she asked.

"I feel it in my heart."

Liv bobbed her head, trying to fully understand his words. It didn't make sense that he still felt so connected to his mate if she had no soul, did it?

Jason turned away. "That's enough chat for today. Get some rest, landlover. I'll be back for you at sunset."

"Can't wait." She entered the cabin and closed the door, wondering if she might be able to sneak off and find Dana. It sounded like Jason was going to get some sleep.

Liv peeked out the curtains of the small living room and there was Jason standing right in front of the window, with his big arms crossed over his chest, frowning. "Get some sleep, landlover," he ordered. "I'm not going anywhere."

Dammit.

CHAPTER EIGHT

Later in the evening, after a long day of pacing and nerves and trying to get a little sleep, Jason came to collect Liv and take her to the great hall, where the festivities were already underway.

Why in the world do they call this "great"? Liv thought the moment they entered the jagged stone entrance. The only thing great about it was—okay, nothing was great about it. It was a big, dark, damp cavern with a high ceiling and a dismal fireplace that did absolutely nothing to fight the frigid temperature. The walls, all solid rock, dripped with that strange "sacred water," which flowed into little channels along the edges of the floor toward an eerily glowing green pool in the back furthest from the entrance.

Jason pulled Liv through the dense crowd of nearly naked men, who stood to the edges of the room, facing Roen's throne—a wooden chair with a sea serpent carved into the high back. The women stood behind him in a long line, each "guest" wearing the same style white outfit like before.

Liv tugged at the top of her dress and tried her best to ignore the tightening in her chest. She felt Roen's gaze from across the room. She wanted to run to him and warn him what was coming, but she'd already gone over this twenty times in her head today. She had to stick to the plan.

Liv's eyes went to work searching for Dana. Thankfully, she wasn't among any of the women. So where the hell was she?

Liv turned to Jason. "Where's my sister?" she whispered.

"Shhh… It's about to start," said a man to her other side.

Her eyes traveled up, up, up the wall of muscles and scarred skin to find Lyle looking down at her. A shiver rippled through her nervous system. Lyle's face looked very similar to Roen's—chiseled jaw, high cheekbones, and full lips—only he wore a full beard and had dark long hair. He also had a few inches on his brother in every direction.

Liv stared up at the seven-foot man, masking her fear. Everything about him said "Danger. If you see this man, run the other way."

"Hello, Lyle. Nice to see you again," she said.

"Only my family calls me Lyle. You may refer to me as L'isle, my traditional merman name." He pulled his stern gaze away and directed it toward a woman—a thin blonde who couldn't be older than twenty—who'd stepped forward and now stood beside Roen's throne. Two men moved from the crowd to the center of the room, where they removed the cloths around their waists.

Liv's stomach tightened into a sick ball. *Oh shit. No.* She didn't want to watch this. Liv turned away.

"Liv, they're only penises," Jason whispered in her ear. "And it's disrespectful not to watch."

Liv had seen so many large merman penises last night that when she'd grabbed a few hours of sleep in the morning, she dreamed they'd formed their own country and started demanding rights. It was pretty weird. "I don't give a crap about the nudity. I'm not watching two men kill each other."

"Only one man will do the killing," he pointed out. "And they don't always die. Some just get really close, and we can save them."

"And those who aren't saved?" she whispered over her shoulder.

"Hey, the maids gotta eat, too." He chuckled.

Liv wanted to vomit. These people were so barbaric.

"Begin." Liv heard Roen's voice call out.

The sound of grunting and fists hitting bone filled the air.

Oh god. Oh god.

Then a wail prompted Liv to cup her hands over her ears. She couldn't listen. Then within the span of a few seconds, the room exploded with cheers.

Jason tapped her shoulder, and Liv removed her hands.

"It's done; you can look now," he said.

Liv glanced over her shoulder toward the center of the room, where a man lay flat on his back, out cold. The other man—with short brown hair and fish-scale tattoos from the neck down—victoriously shook his fists toward the sky.

"Oh crap. Is he okay?" Liv asked.

Jason smiled. "Nope. Too bad. I really liked the guy."

Liv winced. The man was dead. Dead. And everyone was behaving as if he'd lost a boxing match or arm-wrestling contest.

A few men dragged the dead guy outside, and the winner escorted the woman to the other side of the room. She beamed up at the guy like she'd won a brand-new car.

Roen stood from his throne, clapping. He wore his standard suede, nothing else, and looked like a damned sex god with his bronzed skin, sculpted lean muscles, and rippling washboard stomach. His hair, a rich brown made of golds and chestnut hues, fell down around his face, giving him a wicked, fierce look. Liv was in the process of pushing her desires down a deep, dark hole when Roen looked in her direction.

"You're up." Jason gave her a little shove toward Roen.

This is it. Keep calm. Whatever happens, keep calm. Her heart and stomach, however, were in a violent tailspin.

Roen locked eyes on her like a hungry predator and then gave her a cold nod. She nodded back and then stood at his side where the other woman had been.

“Those who wish to place their claim, please step inside the circle,” Roen said, his deep, authoritative voice bouncing off the dark gray stone walls.

The room fell into a tension-filled silence. Not one man stepped forward.

“Last call,” Roen repeated. “Any man who wishes to place a claim, please step into the circle.”

Not only didn’t anyone step forward, she noticed some of the men stepping away, repelled by her. They really believed she was defective or…rejected…or whatever Jason had called her.

“I place my claim.” In strutted Shane.

Oh shit. Where’s Dana? Liv guessed that Shane had her stashed close by in case Liv decided not to play things his way.

“Liv, nice to see you again,” Shane said and dipped his head. Liv didn’t dare look at Roen. She knew he might see right through her.

“Shane.” Liv smiled pleasantly.

“Per our laws,” Roen spoke to Shane, “you are the only man here who wishes to claim this female. Therefore, she is yours.”

What? Liv’s shock almost gave her away, but Shane made no effort to hide his. His face turned bright red, and his hands balled into tight trembling fists.

“Something the matter, Shane?” Roen asked.

Yeah, he wanted a fight and didn’t get one.

Roen continued, “You look disappointed. Of course, I would be too if I’d just claimed another man’s discarded female, but who am I to judge?”

The room filled with grumbles and laughter.

For a split second, Liv's ego urged her to get upset. Then she realized what Roen was really doing: Turning the tables on Shane by not giving him what he wanted. In fact, he seemed to be egging Shane on. Maybe attacking Roen without cause would land Shane in some sort of hot water?

Mermaid-chow water?

Shane made a stiff little bow in Roen's direction and then grabbed Liv's hand before turning away to go take their place with the other couple.

Liv couldn't believe it. Roen hadn't lifted a finger for her. No, she wasn't mad. She was relieved. Her plan had worked.

"There's just one thing," Shane said loudly for all to hear before facing Roen again.

"Yes, Shane?" Roen's voice made it clear he held zero esteem for this man.

"Well," Shane scratched his scruffy black stubble, "I really am an old-school kind of merman."

"And?" Roen crossed his meaty arms over his broad chest.

"I like to adhere to the traditions of our forefathers. I think it shows respect to honor the ancient ways. I will claim my female here for all to see."

Liv's stomach made a little flip, and she jerked her hand away. *Oh God.* Shane had a plan B. Did Roen?

Shane went on, a snide smile glued to his face, "I think it will be a nice way to kick off the evening; show everyone how it's done. A good bite to make her scream, and a good fuck to make her scream louder."

Even the other men, who exchanged glances, seemed uncomfortable with this.

Roen stepped forward, his face filled with a calm, deadly coldness. "You're saying you wish to humiliate the woman, and that is not allowed."

Shane turned to Liv. "You won't mind, will you, darling?"

Liv's mouth opened, but it took a few moments for her to speak. "Um—um…no. That's fine, if it will make Shane happy."

"See," Shane said, "she's all for it."

Shane grabbed Liv's hand and stepped around Roen.

Oh fuck. This plan had gone terribly, terribly wrong.

Shane walked her over to Roen's throne, and he gave her a little push. "Lean forward, honey. I think I'll get us warmed up before the bite."

Liv felt the tears welling in her eyes, and her knees shook so hard, she could barely stand. There was no way she could let him do this. No way. But then Dana would be put up for grabs next and then what?

Liv flinched when Shane placed his hand on her shoulder. The other hand reached down, sliding up her dress.

Liv began to twist away when Roen's loud, restrained voice called out, "Shane, you can have the throne. It's yours."

Shane released her and turned.

"Yes," Roen said. "You heard me right. It's yours. I give it to you."

"You can't *give* me leadership. Giving is for pussies. It is the way of the weak."

"I can," Roen replied with a deep menacing tone, "because there is no law prohibiting my right to do so if I choose." Roen threw out his arms. "So it's yours. All I ask in return is to allow Liv and her sister to leave the island."

Shane smiled. "I knew you didn't have it in you to fight for her." Liv knew Shane referred to the island, not herself. "Because you're weak."

Roen shrugged. "If showing mercy is weak, I guess I am. I simply don't see the point of taking advantage of a female or blackmailing her to do my bidding. Although that seems to be your way and the way of this island—using our mates against us. Just like the island has done to our people for thousands of years. We fight to protect her; she uses our hearts and women to enslave us. But we have a choice to say no. There are other ways to protect the island and they don't involve watching our women suffer."

"We won't get them back if we don't do as she asks," said one man in the crowd.

"You really think the island plans to give them back?" Roen's voice filled the vacuous chamber while he pivoted, addressing the men. "By my calculations, there are over two thousand maids. Two thousand. Yet there are only two hundred of us, including some who've yet to find mates. So you do the math, gentlemen. How many will ever live to see the day when our women are set free? The answer is none. Because we end up dying in these archaic rituals only to be replaced by a new harvest of warriors. We fight. We love. And we die. But we are never allowed to live. So make no mistake, we are the island's slaves, and she has no plans to change that. But I do. So you may follow Shane as leader of the island and continue accepting these antiquated traditions meant to control us, or you can follow me—not as the island's chosen leader, but as *your* leader."

"The island will punish us," screamed a random male voice.

Roen lifted his chin and moved his steady, confident gaze over the faces in the room. "She's already punishing us, and if I do nothing about it, my sons will be next." He pointed to Liv, who at this point was sure she'd stopped breathing. "And Liv, my mate—not my discarded claim—will face centuries of serving the island."

The room filled with loud grumbles and voices.

"Don't listen to him!" Shane yelled, his face a furious shade of red. "Our people are strong because of the island. And our ways keep her protected. The time of the Dorans is over. He's weak. He's afraid."

No one seemed to give a crap about anything he said. They were too busy debating with each other over what Roen had proposed.

"You must decide now, men." Roen's deep, magnetic voice cut right through the noise. "It will not be an easy journey, but we will make it if we stick together."

A small group of extremely rude-looking men, wearing red cloths, broke away from the crowd and faced Roen. "We will follow you. We are not afraid to face the island."

Then it was like a domino effect. One by one, the rest of the men did the same. All except Shane and his gang of about ten.

"Roen, Roen, Roen…" they began chanting his name. The walls rumbled and the floors shook violently. At first, Liv thought their deep, loud voices caused it; however, she realized it was the island answering back.

She sounds really pissed.

When Liv opened her mouth to suggest the party move outside before the mountain came crashing down on their heads, Shane turned and grabbed her by the throat, slamming her backward into the ground. A horrible pain racked her body, and her vision blacked out for a moment.

"Liv!" Roen yelled out, and the room fell silent.

Shane snarled viciously, "There are no rules against killing a landlover for fun, so let's see how brave he is without you." Shane squeezed, and in that moment, Lyle smashed his fist into Shane's face. He fell unconscious to the side.

Roen reached her, his eyes filled with panic. "Liv? Can you hear me?"

Liv couldn't breathe let alone speak.

"Someone bring water!" Roen turned back to Liv. "Just relax, Liv. You'll be okay."

A man showed up with a glass bottle, and Roen quickly shoved it to Liv's lips. She tried to swallow, but it wouldn't go down.

"All you need is a few drops," Roen said, "and you'll be fine. Try to drink it."

That wasn't true. While the water did work on her, it didn't have the same effect as it did on everyone else. She seemed to need a lot more to produce minor results. It was why they said Liv was "defective."

The room began blinking out.

"Drink, Liv," Roen commanded, "or I'll throw you into that pool."

What? No! Liv's air returned to her, and she pushed Roen's hand away. "I'm fine," she whispered. "He just knocked the wind out of me."

Roen smiled at her, brushing the hair back from her forehead. "Thank God. You scared the hell out of me." He looked over his shoulder at Lyle. "Put Shane into a holding cell. Make sure his men join him."

Lyle gave the nod, and the men from Shane's little band of thugs were immediately seized and dragged off.

"What about the women?" Lyle said in Roen's ear, loud enough for Liv to hear.

Roen shook his head. "Send them to their cabins. There will be no more claimings. Not today, not ever, if I can help it."

Lyle nodded and started directing the men to take the "guests" away.

Liv smiled and looked up into Roen's beaming green eyes. "You had a plan B."

CHAPTER NINE

After telling his men he'd return shortly to discuss the next steps, Roen grabbed Liv to return her to the cottage. He insisted on carrying her, and she didn't protest. After everything that had happened, there was no place better than Roen's arms.

They moved along a dark path through the forest, and his touch literally made her feel like she might burst wide open with joy because they were together now and a light shined brightly at the end of the tunnel for them all.

"This was a bad idea," he grumbled. The man's body buzzed like a giant bumblebee—something that happened when these mermen became aroused. "I should've asked Lyle to take you."

Liv snuggled her cheek against his bare, hot chest, feeling dopy. "I don't think so."

"Well, I know so." He set her down. "Here's your cottage. I'll have Dana brought shortly." The faint outdoor lights of the cottage caught Roen's handsome face. Those plump, sinful lips, that masculine jawline covered in a short growth of whiskers, those fierce…*angry eyes?*

Of course he is. You were horrible to him.

"Roen," she reached for his hand and gave it a soft squeeze, "I'm sorry about earlier. I'm sorry for lying to you."

He stepped back a little, remaining silent for several long moments, his eyes fixed to the ground. Finally, he said, "You should've trusted me with the truth."

Maybe, but… "I didn't want Shane to hurt you or Dana. I did what I thought was right."

"Lucky for me, you're a terrible liar. Goodbye, Liv," he said briskly and turned down the flagstone walkway away from the cottage.

"Roen, wait." She ran after him and grabbed his arm. "Is that it? Just goodbye?"

"What else would it be? Welcome home? This island is not safe for you. It never was and it never will be. Especially now that the fight for control has begun, which is why I must go and see to it the island allows you all to leave."

"You're going to ask the island's permission? Isn't she going to be a little upset with you right now?" Roen had incited a rebellion against her.

"She may be upset, but letting the women leave is in her best interest since we've refused to claim them and there is a limit to how long humans can remain."

"Why? What happens to us?"

"Not to you—to the island. This is a closed ecosystem. Your presence is disruptive, like a virus that weakens the body."

Ah yes. The wonderfully informative pamphlet had mentioned that. "So we make her sick." Liv wanted to laugh.

"Something like that."

"The feeling is mutual."

"I'm sure she's aware. Which is why she'll want you all gone as quickly as possible. It's for the greater good."

Liv did not share Roen's point of view. Because the island would do whatever the damned hell she pleased, when it damn well pleased her, despite the impact on the people. For Christ's sake, look what the crazy bitch did to their women. Liv also didn't believe for a moment that old Crazy Dirt would let Liv stroll out of there without Roen having to pay a price. Of course, Roen wouldn't tell her that, because she wouldn't approve.

Liv swatted a giant bug circling near her face. "What are you going to give up this time?"

"What do you mean?"

Couldn't they go inside and talk? The bugs were out in droves tonight, though they stayed clear of Roen. Probably too afraid. "I know how this works. She'll want something from you to let me go."

"Allowing you to leave is in her best interest, too."

Astonished, Liv tilted her head. "Wait. You just delivered a scalding reprimand because I lied to you about Shane. So why don't you be a true leader and set the example—cut the crap and tell me why she's going to let me paddle away for a second time when all of the other mates are used as leverage against their men."

Roen ran both hands down his face.

"Roen, there is absolutely no way for either of us to get through this if we don't trust each other."

"This," he dropped his hands, "is the issue: You don't trust me. You push back and you snarl and you think you know what's best, when you are a landlover incapable of understanding this world or its true importance."

Liv's mouth fell wide open for several moments while she bit back her anger. "Okay. I've had about enough of the condescending mer-machismo, buddy. I may not be seven feet tall and have big fat bulging biceps, but I assure you my brain is as evolved as yours—if not more because I don't have to share it with a big fat penis. So why don't you go find yourself a pair of pants, put them on, and tell me why the island would *ever* let me walk out of here instead of dropping a tree on my head just to punish you?"

Roen kicked a little pebble with his bare foot off the pathway.

"You want me to cooperate and trust you?" she pushed. "This is the time, big man."

Roen made a deep grumble. He knew she was right and it killed him. "Separating mates drives them mad. If you leave, it will only serve to weaken me—she gets her wish to watch me lose."

Jason had mentioned that little part about going crazy. "I still don't understand. The first time she let me go, it was a trade so you'd lead. Now she'll want me to leave to hurt you?" she asked.

"Because the first time—" He stopped speaking.

"What?" she pushed.

Roen turned his head away. "A merman rarely gives his heart to anyone, even his mate. It's what keeps us from becoming too vulnerable."

"And?"

"And I promised I'd give mine to her." He then looked into her eyes and despite the faint light, Liv saw a flicker of deep emotion. "I wasn't able to do it."

"Oh." Liv could hardly breathe. Did that mean Roen's heart was already taken? Because hers sure the hell was. "I'm guessing she wasn't happy?"

"No. For her, it's always about domination, winning and losing—the strong triumphing over the weak either mentally or physically. It's like a religion to her."

"Then let her win. Admit weakness and leave with me."

"She'd never allow me to walk away. Even if she did, I made a commitment to end this and bring back these men's women. I can't leave things like they are and permit the suffering to continue."

This was why Liv couldn't help her feelings for Roen. He wouldn't back down from a fight no matter how harrowing the odds. Still, it worried her. What if he died? What if she left and never saw him again? The thought broke her heart.

"What if I want to stay?" she asked, gently placing her hand on his arm.

"I won't allow it. And you'd be nothing but a distraction not to mention leverage for Shane's men. They know I have feelings for you."

Liv felt a little flutter deep in her chest. He admitted to having feelings for her. Yes, duh, it was obvious. But hearing him say it felt so, so good. *Except, it's not enough to make him want to be with you or believe we'll work out.* That, of course, was her needy voice wanting what it wanted. The other voice inside her head knew he was right. Her being there only made Roen vulnerable. Especially now that he'd admitted she was his mate and fought to protect her yet again.

He added, "And even now as we speak, I'm barely able to keep myself from taking you right here in the dirt. Is that really what you want?"

"Yes!" Liv knew exactly what her body wanted: Him. Naked. Slamming his hard flesh into her over and over again until she died of ecstasy. She couldn't stop thinking about it. As for her heart, it couldn't possibly want him more than it did at this very moment.

He puffed out a breath and shot her a look of disapproval.

"Well," she offered, "it doesn't have to be in the dirt. There's a nice bed inside."

He shook his head. "This is no time for jokes, Liv."

Who's joking? she thought.

He went on, "You now know you are my mate and exactly what that means. Do you think I want to again risk turning you into a maid? Do you understand how lucky you are to have escaped that fate the last time you were here?"

"Well, no. But—"

"But nothing," he cut her off. "You are leaving. I will drive this situation to an end once and forever."

Hearing him say that and thinking of his road ahead made her realize how selfish she was being. Here she was focusing on what she wanted—him—while he worried about saving thousands. "I'm sorry. You're right, Roen. I'm the last thing you need to be worried about."

"I'm glad you finally understand."

That didn't mean she wasn't in the process of feeling like her entire world was caving in around her heart. Because it was. It felt like a cruel, cruel joke to finally be with Roen and hear him admit the truth about his feelings, only to be driven away again.

"So what do you plan to do after I leave?" Another big bug zoomed by and smacked her forehead and she began to wonder if the island was making them do it.

"Read," he replied. "I'm going to read."

"Uh. Okay. Reading is…relaxing."

"No. I have to find a way to free the maids. If I can do that, I can remove the hold the island has over many of the men."

"So you think there's a cure?" This was exciting.

"Our folklore says the island changed us all at one point, giving us legs, and then decided to take them away from our women. The island doesn't have magical powers. She can't wave a wand and change a person into another creature. She is a life force that can communicate, influence, and trigger physiological reactions under certain circumstances."

"You still think she's alive?"

"I *know* she is," he said. "However, she's not a god."

"She can make herself disappear and create storms. She can mutate women into monsters. I'd say that's pretty damned impressive."

The moon suddenly broke through the cloud cover and shined brightly on Roen's face. She'd never seen a more determined expression in his eyes, like the man was mentally preparing for war.

Maybe because he is. And the thought frightened her.

"Her abilities can always be explained by a physical or chemical connection," he said. "She manipulates her chemistry and generates heat deep inside the ground. When she does, the moisture releases from the top of that mountain or vents around the island. It creates a mirage of sorts, reflecting the sun and the water back at whomever is looking at her. If anyone gets close enough, she has the means to create vibrations that liquefy the beach. In the case of the maids, she cannot transform a person merely by willing it. A catalyst is required."

Liv felt like a child who'd been allowed backstage at a magic show. And there she'd been, believing that the magician really could make himself disappear. Now that strange orange or blue sky made perfect sense. The island had developed a sort of camouflaging ability like a chameleon or that color-changing octopus she'd once seen on the Nature Channel. There were hundreds if not thousands of examples of this in nature.

Still, despite not being magic, those abilities were pretty damned impressive.

Roen continued, "There are clear, physical limits to her abilities, which is why she needs us, but that doesn't make her any less dangerous. And it does not negate the fact that she must be protected from the world. Without her, no one lives."

"So how do you plan to bring the women back?" Liv asked.

"I don't know yet. We instinctually bite women before sex, but the transformation only happens to our mates and no other women."

"You bit me and nothing happened," Liv said.

"You're not the norm. You're resistant to whatever is in the water and to our pheromones. We also did not have sex. So you present additional variables."

Roen was dancing dangerously close to science-speak, and it was turning up her thermostat from "sizzling for Roen"—yes, it never stopped—to full-fledged bonfire of formidable lust.

"I can help you, Roen."

"No. You're leaving." Roen took her hand and began pulling her back toward the front door of the cottage. "And I really must go now. The men are waiting."

Yeah. She knew. And the thought of being separated again had already begun to turn her inside out. "I don't have to be here physically," she pointed out, stumbling behind him over the moonlit walkway. "I can take whatever books and records you have. I'm good at figuring out things like this—connections that can't be seen with the naked eye is something I've obsessed over for years. We can Skype once a day and compare notes."

Plus, at least this way she'd know what was going on and see him every day. *While you slowly go mad from being separated.*

Roen stopped directly in front of the door. "Fine. I'll have my men load everything into crates. You can take them with you in the morning."

"In the morning?"

"The sooner you're all gone, the better." He reached for the door handle, twisted, and pushed it open for her.

Liv couldn't move her feet inside. She didn't want to leave him. "I want to stay with you tonight."

"Absolutely not."

"We don't have to have sex." Honestly, at this point, she'd take just being near him for a few more hours. God only knew when or if she'd ever see him again.

"Because I will fuck you and that's not going to help either of us."

Fuck. Simply hearing him say the word evoked X-rated images of her riding his thick, hard shaft, their bodies glistening with sweat, their lips swollen from rough, needy lovemaking.

Liv's toes curled over her leather sandals, and the muscles deep inside her core screamed with the most carnal sexual ache she'd ever experienced. *Dammit, forget the cuddling.* There had to be an XL condom somewhere on this godforsaken island.

"I'm pretty sure it's exactly the sort of help I need, so speak for yourself, Roen."

"Liv, I must be absolutely clear; nothing has changed between us. You and I cannot happen, because even if by some miracle I achieve my goals, someone will need to stay behind and protect this place and everyone knows bad things happen to landlovers here." His voice dropped an octave. "Very. Very bad things."

"Why does that someone need to be you?" she argued.

"Do you suggest I enslave someone else?"

"No. But—"

"But nothing. A leader puts his people first, his family first. And think what you will, but these people are my family. Including those creatures in the water. Good night, Liv." He gave the front door a little push, opening it wider—a sign that the conversation was over.

Fight. Love. Die. That was what Roen had said was their fate back in the great hall. He wanted everyone to have the chance to live a real life. Everyone except himself and her.

She smoothed her hands over her long hair and stepped inside the cottage past Roen and his harsh gaze. *Wait. Don't let him push you away, Liv. You have a say. This is your life, too.*

She turned in a huff. "What'll happen when we're apart if mates who separate go crazy?"

"If I live through this, I will find the solution. One hurdle at a time, Liv."

"So, let me get this straight," she began, seething. "You save the island, stay forever, and I find someone else. That's your plan."

"Yes. Because I *will* find a way to untie this noose around our necks."

Liv felt her heart twist into an angry knot. He considered their relationship to be a noose while she thought their relationship to be a rare and precious gift. So few people got to experience something so powerful.

"And if you don't live through this?" she asked.

"Then you will be free either way," he said solemnly.

So he believed the connection between them would end if he died, even though that wasn't how love worked. Yes, she loved him. She'd known since that day she'd first left him behind on the island, although it took a while to admit it to herself.

"I tried to come back for you, Roen. That morning you freed me from the island. I tried to come back for you. I asked myself what I'd be willing to give up to be with you and save you. The answer was everything."

"What's your point?" he asked.

"The island didn't create what I feel, so you can't 'break' it. And if you don't believe me, just remember you said yourself, I'm immune to her."

"I said you're resistant, not immune. Either way, I'll make sure you move on."

He spoke like he truly believed he could conquer everything and anything if he put his mind to it. *Wrong.*

"Of course," she fumed, "because it's all your choice. Not mine."

"If you wish to put it that way, then yes. It is my choice."

Liv shook her head in frustration. She couldn't take being pushed away from him like this anymore. Whatever had happened in Roen's life with his family and parents had skewed his perception of love. To him it meant placing the protection of the other and sacrificing one's self above everything else. Sadly, it was what she loved about him. Even sadder, it was the reason he felt that pushing her away was the *only* way when there might be other options. He simply felt too scared to even try.

"And if you're wrong, Roen? If I'm not able to move on? What's your plan B then? Because I'll be crazy, and you might be dead."

He shot her a look. She'd definitely hit a nerve. "That won't happen."

"How can you be so sure?"

"Because I never fail."

What a stubborn, egotistical man! She could argue and push and plead, but once again he'd put her in a situation where he gave her no say. "You've already failed, Roen. Because you're a giant ass!"

"You dare call me an ass, landlover?"

"Oh, sorry. Mer-ass. And you definitely don't deserve me if you're not willing to fight for me."

She reached to shut the front door, but he pushed it back open with his strong arm and stepped inside, towering over her.

"I did fight for you," he said in a loud, angry voice. "Four times now if I'm counting correctly, which is why you're still alive."

Being so close, feeling the heat of his body, threatened to suck the wind from her angry sails.

"And I'm thankful," she snapped. "I'm also ready to leave in hopes of never seeing you again. So your work here is done, big bad merman."

Roen turned and marched off, blistering with anger, swiping at branches while he grumbled away, "Damned landlover women. So goddamned ungrateful."

"Coward!" she yelled out the door. "That's what you all are! Mer-chickens of the sea! Who run away with their tails between their legs!"

"We don't have tails, woman!" he screamed back from a distance.

"Yeah!" she hollered back. "I noticed. And who the *hell* ever heard of a merman without a goddamned tail, huh?" Liv slammed the door shut and flipped on the lights, immediately marching to the little table in the corner to pour herself a tall glass of scotch.

Stubborn asshole. Just tosses me over like an old rusty boat anchor. Noose, my ass. He's the noose. Stupid ocean-Neanderthal. She gulped down the smoky hot liquid and then held back a gag. The burn was almost unbearable and the taste was frigging awful. What did a girl have to do around here to get a good bottle of Russian River Pinot? Huh? *Oh, but nooo. Mermen drink hard alcohol, wear skirts, and throw boat parties.*

"Liv?"

Dana stood in the front doorway, looking confused as ever, her wide brown eyes filled with fear.

"Dana, ohmygod." Liv put down her glass, rushed forward, and hugged Dana tightly.

"What's going on, Liv?"

Liv let go and placed her hand on Dana's cheek. "What's going on is that you're safe. And I'm taking you home tomorrow."

"I don't want to go home, Liv; I want to stay here with Shane."

Liv couldn't believe her ears. "No, baby, you don't."

"Oh, yes. I do. In fact, I want to stay here with all of them. They need me. And they're all really, really hot. Have you seen them naked? Have you?" Dana held out her hands a few feet apart to make her point.

"Dana—" Liv gripped her shoulders firmly "—what you feel is a result of their pheromones or something. It makes you high and feel stupid-happy, so you don't realize that they only want to use you and hurt you. What you feel isn't real."

"I saw the way you looked at Roen while you were fighting. Are you saying that's not real either?"

"Yes, it's real. That's because Roen and I have a special relationship that…" *Ugh. This is stupid.* "No. I'm sorry. You're right; it's not real, which is why I'm leaving with you tomorrow."

Dana looked at her feet. "I don't want to go, Liv."

"Dana, you're not thinking straight. Because if you were, you'd be begging to get the hell off this rock."

"Then why do I feel so—"

"Mom and Dad love you, Dana. Krista loves you. And so do I. So if you can't believe me about what you're feeling, can you at least believe in that?" She would never understand why Dana felt more to her like a daughter than a younger sister. It might've had to do with the fact that when Dana was a baby, Liv spent hours rocking her and pretending she was hers. Of course, they were only five years apart and with their similar faces, long dark hair, and big brown eyes, they looked more like twins than anything else. Regardless, Liv felt fiercely protective of her baby sister.

Dana nodded. "I know you love me, but can't I—"

"Good. Because I promise once we get far, far away from here, you'll see things in another light."

Liv also prayed that Dana went back to being that smart, sassy, independent sister she loved so much. This version was so damned annoying.

Chapter Ten

Early the next morning, a loud knock on the front door woke Liv. Her hair a tangled mess from tossing and turning all night, she slowly rolled from the king-size bed in the cozy bedroom, where Dana still slept, and went to answer, finding a handwritten note shoved under the front door. It informed them the boat would be leaving soon, and reminded everyone of the law prohibiting the women from speaking of their time on the island or of its inhabitants.

Should you break this law, the punishment will be swift and not limited to yourself.

The scary-as-hell part was that this threat wasn't idle. The island *had* known when Liv broke the promise. And yes, the punishment had been swift and not limited to herself—she'd ended up having a seizure-like episode on the floor of her psychiatrist's office and then, that same day, Dana experienced a similar episode, almost dying from asphyxiation right before her eyes in the ER. Miraculously—or more accurately put: suspiciously—Liv had a small vial of sacred water in her purse and used it to save Dana.

The thing was, Liv had no clue how the island had done it—getting to Dana—especially considering what Roen had said. The island's reach was limited to things around her that she could react with or connect to.

Liv woke Dana, and they washed up. Neither had any belongings to pack since they'd been "invited" as "guests" Wild West style. After grabbing an apple and some bottled water from the small kitchen inside the cottage, Liv and Dana marched down the hill along the dirt path. The sun was just over the horizon, and the sky shimmered with electric blue.

Liv stared through the swaying treetops at the unnatural display. Love this place or hate it, the beauty was unlike anything on the rest of the planet.

"You see that?" Liv said to Dana while the two made their way toward the marina.

Dana said nothing. Liv could tell from the lack of conversation and Dana's sagging posture that she felt horrible. Maybe her merman-contact high had worn off.

Either way, Dana wasn't arguing about leaving and they'd soon be on their way home.

One by one, the women quietly filed onto the small cruise ship, looking like they'd all been the victims of a spring break tequila-drinking contest.

Guess the penis-ogling party is over, girls. Despite glum appearances, Liv knew these women had lucked out. Big time. They'd all go home, see their families, forget about this place—or not—and move on.

Some of the women disappeared to their cabins, while others gathered on the deck to quietly stare at the island, looking confused as hell. Maybe they wondered where they were or why the last week or so felt like a strange dream.

Liv, on the other hand, felt nothing but pain in her chest. She might never see Roen again, and their final words hadn't been nice ones. She didn't want it to end like that, but she'd be damned to be talked down to and told "what was best" for her. The final slap was that no one delivered the books Roen mentioned. He didn't want her help. He didn't want anything to do with her.

Fine. I'm done begging. I'm done pining for him. And if I go crazy, well, then…that's that. Of course, it was a fat lie because what came next would be restless nights and days filled with heartache. Being apart from Roen mentally and physically pained her.

Did she believe Roen would find a way to change that? No. Only she could decide when she'd be ready to let go. And that wouldn't be for a very, very long time. *Maybe never.* She genuinely loved him.

The ship slowly pulled away from the harbor, and Liv and Dana stood at the railing, gazing out at the island while more and more came into view.

What the hell? Liv could scarcely believe her eyes. *These men don't wear shoes or clothes half the time, yet they have a fancy communication tower?* The metal structure was loaded with satellite dishes and stood right next to a giant green water tower. *That explains the fantastic water pressure.* And on top of all those beautifully modern bungalows peppering the forest, solar panels covered every roof. *And that explains all of their electricity.*

This place is too damned weird for words.

The boat pulled out of the marina, and Liv turned her back, taking a deep breath and praying she'd be strong enough to get through whatever came next.

One hurdle at a time, Liv, she said in her head, mocking Roen's deep, cocky tone.

All of a sudden, a woman's scream filled the air. As Liv turned her head, looking for the source, someone shoved her over the railing into the water.

Oh God. Oh God. There wasn't enough time to feel the cold water or care about who'd pushed her over. Because when Liv's head made it to the surface, the scene of horror was worse than anything she could imagine. Hundreds of coalmine black bodies with long tails scaled the sides of the ship, digging their powerful claws right into the steel. From her angle in the water, she couldn't see what was happening atop, but the bloodcurdling yells were enough.

"Dana!" Liv screamed, and bloody bodies began raining down as mermaids tossed them over.

"Dana!" Liv screamed again. She had no way up to the boat to get Dana. "You fucking bitches! I'll kill you! You hear me! Don't you fucking touch her!"

Ohmygod. This isn't happening. This isn't happening. Liv had said those words to herself too many times, and now she knew better. This was happening. It was the island's doing.

"You can't have her," Liv screamed.

"Liv!" Dana's voice called out from behind her.

Treading water, Liv spun and spotted Dana. A huge, hungry-looking mermaid gripped Dana by a big clump of her long dark hair. It opened its mouth, displaying sharp white teeth, and reached for Dana's neck.

Liv yelled, "Let her go or I will kill you! Do you hear me? I will hunt you and kill you. I swear it!"

The maid blinked her big yellow eyes at Liv, freezing mid-bite.

"Let her go," Liv growled protectively.

The maid released its prize and slowly sank into the water, its gaze fixed on Liv the entire way.

Oh shit. Was that thing coming after her now?

Liv didn't care. As long as Dana got out, that was all that mattered.

"Liv! Liv! Help!" Dana fought to keep her head above water.

Liv swam to Dana and started pulling her toward the pier.

"I saw one of those things coming right at you," Dana panted. "I pushed you and jumped in, but I hit my arm on the way down. I think I broke it."

She'd probably hit a damned mermaid. *Hope Dana broke its head.*

The boom of loud male voices echoed through the air and men started appearing on the dock. However, instead of jumping into the water to help Liv and Dana, they stood there, mouths hanging open, staring at the massacre on the ship.

"Liv!" Roen pushed his way through the men, almost knocking one into the water. The man scrambled back, doing everything in his power not to go in.

"Roen!" She struggled to keep her head above water while towing Dana with one arm hooked underneath her shoulder.

"Liv!" Roen yelled again, a look of pure panic on his face. With the shrill cries of the mermaids and the screams of the women, who were being torn to shreds and tossed into the water, he hadn't heard her.

"Roen!" Liv yelled again.

This time, she caught his attention, and when he spotted her in the water, he took a small breath. For the second time in her life, Roen looked at her like she was his most precious possession, and it made her insides flutter and roll.

A cry from an injured woman with a deep gash in her neck rang out in the water behind her.

Roen ordered three reluctant men into the water and then dove in head first. Faster than her brain could register, Roen's men were to the woman and Dana, pulling them to safety. No doubt about it, these guys were powerful swimmers. Roen followed and grabbed her arm, wrapping it around his neck. He swam to the pier, towing her on his back.

The rest of the men, who'd remained on the dock, reached down and lifted her out followed by Roen.

She rushed over to Dana, who sat panting, cradling her arm. The injured woman had been laid out on her back, and one of the men removed the cloth around his waist to apply pressure to the bleeding wound.

"Bring her water," Roen commanded.

Dana glanced at the woman. "Ohmygod. That's Cindy." Dana rushed over and kneeled beside the petite woman, brushing her long blonde wet hair from her forehead. "You're going to be all right," Dana said. Meanwhile, the bloodcurdling screams continued a hundred meters away.

"Do something," Liv yelled at the men.

Roen squeezed her shoulder and shook his head remorsefully. "We cannot."

"What? Yes, you can. Stop them," Liv argued.

"We are no match for the maids. Even if we were, no one would want to risk killing another man's mate."

Liv suddenly understood the sad, horrifying truth of the situation. She closed her eyes and held back her tears.

"Don't listen," Dana said to the injured woman. "Just listen to my voice. Nothing else matters."

The woman passed out.

"Roen," Liv said, "she's going to die."

He nodded. "Let's get her to the great hall." He snapped his fingers at one of the men, who scooped the woman into his arms. Like a giant blur, the man was gone.

"Wait!" Dana yelled and went running after them, hugging her injured arm.

Liv was about to follow when Roen gripped her shoulder, looking nervous. "We'll catch up; you stay with me." He took Liv's hand and pulled her along.

Liv instantly felt safer and calmer just from his touch.

"Roen," she panted, noticing that her clothes dripped with blood-tinged seawater, "what the hell is happening? Why did they attack?"

Not stopping his brisk pace, he said, "Because they can, since they're able to tolerate sunlight all of a sudden."

"Why do you think it's sudden? One of the maids I saw the morning I left here was out in sunlight."

Roen abruptly halted, and though Liv thought she'd run right into him, he had her by the shoulders before she could blink. "What do you mean, Liv?"

"The mermaid who made me promise never to tell about the island stood in the sun—the others ran away."

"Why didn't you tell me this?" he shouted.

"I don't know. I thought you knew, and the detail didn't seem important after watching those things devour a man in front of my face."

"A non-nocturnal mermaid didn't seem important?"

Liv pulled her hand from his firm grasp. "Don't—" she pointed her finger in his face "—you raise your voice to me, Roen. Not ever. Or I swear to God I will hurt you somewhere special."

"You can't hurt me. I'm a merman."

"Oh, for God's sake, Roen! Stop with the Superman crap!"

"Not Superman. Mer. Man," he corrected. "Superman is fictional. Mermen are real. Don't ever forget that," he growled.

"How could I forget when you guys are the reason my sister's life almost ended three minutes ago? Or when I got kidnapped from my home? Or held against my will and had my neck almost snapped by one of you? Trust me, I know. So you'll have to excuse me, Mr. High and Mighty Merman, but I've been a little busy trying to survive, not go crazy, and protect my sister. So don't you dare blame me for this massacre because I failed to mention that one of your horrifying women went for a morning swim in sunlight."

Roen's harsh expression melted away, and he looked down at the ground. "My apologies. I'm upset, not to mention worried." He raised his head and looked at her with those stunning green eyes. "I needed to know you were safe and far away from here, given what comes next. Now, I'm not sure what I'll do."

Now Liv felt bad. "What comes next?"

He bit his full, sensual bottom lip. "I will answer your question—I promise—but let's check on the woman and Dana first. Then we may speak."

"Yes. You're right." What the hell was she thinking?

They continued on the trail that wove between pine trees with trunks five feet in diameter, and Liv immediately noticed something different about the air.

"Roen," she said, barely keeping up with his pace, "what the hell is that?"

"What?"

"The temperature is getting warmer."

"And?"

"The air on this island always gets colder the closer you get to the mountain." It made sense if Crazy Dirt—aka the island—directed her heat to shield herself from the outside world.

Roen slowed for a moment, then returned to his brisk pace. "I don't foking know, though you're right, something's off."

That was not the answer she expected to hear from Roen.

When they reached the mouth of the cavern—aka the "great" hall—Liv expected to see the woman fully recuperated, but one of Roen's men shoved past them from behind with a bottle in his hand. The moment he reached her body on the floor, he poured the liquid into her mouth. "Drink it down," he said softly. "Everything will be fine."

Roen stood frozen in the jagged stone doorway, tightly gripping Liv's hand.

The man holding the woman's head looked up at Roen and shook his head in grief. "It's too late. She's dead."

Dana, who'd been standing and watching, began to cry.

"Why didn't you give her water from the…" Roen's words died. "Goddammit."

Liv's eyes followed Roen's gaze and noticed the empty pool of water. The night before it had been full and glowing with an eerie green light.

"Where'd it all go?" she said.

Roen released her hand and rubbed his face, groaning.

"Roen?"

"There's no more sacred water," he said.

"I see that. Why? Is the island dead?" Roen had once told her that the island was like a fearful child. And that child kept having nightmares about the landlovers coming to take away all of her water. Unfortunately, that water was like her blood, so while she could give away some, she couldn't live without it altogether.

Roen closed his eyes and tilted his face toward the soaring ceiling. After several moments, he shook his head. "She is angry, not dead."

"Are you sure?" Liv asked.

"Yes, I can hear her heartbeat and feel her bitterness in the air."

"Oh. She's bitter?" Liv yelled at Roen. "She tried to kill Dana and me, and about fifty women just became a mermaid banquet!"

Roen released a frustrated breath. "There is no turning back now. We must see this through to the end as our scriptures state."

Liv wasn't familiar with their scriptures, but it didn't take a genius to know that some sort of doom-related milestone had been reached. "That sounds bad."

"At least this will all come to an end one way or another."

Liv searched in his eyes for an answer that wasn't there. "Even us?"

"You and I never had a chance to begin with." He brushed his thumb over her bottom lip and his eyes filled with deep sorrow. "Even if it's what my heart has always wanted."

Chapter Eleven

Later that morning, after the island's healer, Holden, confirmed Dana had a fractured arm and gave her a few drops of water, which worked immediately—*Guess she's not "defective"*—Roen and a few of his men brought them back to his home. His mansion, built in a log-cabin style resembling something one might find in Aspen, sat atop a forested hill with large panoramic windows and a pitched roof. Inside, however, was anything but rustic. The smooth white walls, large oil paintings, and modern furniture with crisp fabrics and sharp angles made the home feel more like a posh New York penthouse. Not that she'd ever been in one, but who didn't watch *House Hunters*?

The funny part was, Roen had called the place "pedestrian." It was a reminder he'd once lived in a different world where money was no object. Private planes, expensive suits, and chauffeurs. He'd sacrificed it all for her and to help these people. He was a natural-born protector, and it was what she loved about him.

Since the attack on the boat, however, Roen seemed nervous and unsettled, not at all like the protector Roen she knew. "Don't you let anyone *foking* near her," he'd yelled at the guards before leaving, "or I swear I will rip out your hearts."

She wondered if the man might actually be cracking. *Good. He can join me.*

Now, what did he plan to do regarding her and Dana? She suspected he hadn't made up his mind.

Or doesn't know. Leaving by boat was too risky, and flying out, considering the island's "air control" capabilities, wasn't a winner either. They might find themselves getting cooked right out of the sky.

The only thing Liv knew for certain? Roen wouldn't throw in the towel when he wanted something. Right now, he wanted her gone. Far the hell away from him. Maybe even more so now that things had heated up.

Island vs. Mermen. Sounded like a damned B-movie. And a slaughter waiting to happen. Roen mentioned once that the island could read their hearts. So without secrecy, how would they ever get the upper hand in a fight? Their giant muscles would be useless, like bringing a maraca to a gun fight.

The only real option might be to stand against *La Gran Perra*, refuse to do her evil bidding, and weather any punishment she doled out. A battle of the wills between two species that excelled at digging in and taking heads.

That did not sound enjoyable.

Which brought Liv to her second mind-boggling question: If pushed to fight team merman, what would be the island's weapon?

Love. Love is her biggest weapon. Plain and simple. These men loved those…things in the water and Crazy Dirt used them as leverage. Exactly why Roen's move to "cure" the maids was key.

I can help with that. She could figure out how the island triggered the transformation.

Yay. Something to do aside from feeling scared or horny.

With Dana still sleeping, Liv took a shower to rinse away the sheen of dried salt and blood from her skin and then changed into a black stretchy dress she'd found in the closet. There were stacks in every size along with black leather sandals, too. *Guess they buy in bulk, a* thought that mildly disturbed her, knowing they were for the comfort of the female "guests."

She went downstairs and wandered through Roen's modern palace, still finding it hard to believe this kind of luxury existed out in the middle of the North Pacific while remaining hidden from the world.

Liv passed the doorway of the formal dining room with seating for fifty plus, and then walked along a brightly lit hallway lined with life-sized oil paintings. Her first time inside this house, she'd been so frightened by the situation she hadn't taken time to appreciate the art.

She strolled along slowly, noting each painting and their historical significance—battles; a mermaid dying on a rock while her human-looking lover wept; a commanding man with long hair, summoning waves with a trident on a stormy night.

One in particular, an abstract of shadows swimming in the ocean away from the island, caught her attention. With the bold brushstrokes and colors, she couldn't be sure, but the silhouettes seemed masculine.

Liv stepped back, focusing on the textures of the picture. Yes, the shadows in the water were men, and the figures standing in the shadows of the trees, watching the men swim away, were women. With legs.

Liv made a mental note to ask Roen about the painting and then continued to the end of the hallway toward a set of bright blue double doors painted with tribal mermaid symbols.

She knocked and cautiously poked her head inside when no one answered.

"Wow." Roen said he'd been spending his time reading and had more to do. Now she understood why. This wasn't a room but the Merman National Library.

Or is it an aquarium? At the entrance stood a floor-to-ceiling saltwater fish tank, like something found at Sea World, holding several spotted sharks four feet long. Brightly colored fish—blue and orange, black and red—darted in and out between the crevices of black lava rocks placed in the corners. She'd never seen such an enormous tank in someone's home.

Funny, I thought Roen hated fish. Maybe he wanted to make an effort to change. Yeah, she could see him doing that. The man refused to be a slave to anything, including his fears.

Except when those fears come to me. He refused to even look those fears in the eye.

She walked around the aquatic wall, and the full view of the library came into focus. It was all one level that included a spacious sitting area with an old steam trunk for a coffee table, a worn, welcoming brown couch, and a very comfortable burgundy armchair angled toward a fireplace with a giant rusty anchor propped up on the mantle.

No doubt a souvenir from some battle or ship they sank.

She then turned her attention to the four aisles of shelves running to the back of a room the length of half a football field.

Liv wandered down one of the center aisles, her eyes drinking in the floor-to-ceiling rows of thick books.

You look fun. She plucked one off the shelf. It looked especially old with a faded light brown leather jacket and gold, hand-painted numbers on the spine.

Liv opened to the front page, and the musty smell of old paper immediately hit her nose. Careful not to let the acid of her fingers touch any text, she gently flipped the pages by the corners until the word "Doran" caught her eye.

Filled with a great rage, Segar Doran stood like a mighty oak, alone in the dark cold belly of the sacred mountain, a torch in one hand and lifeless mermaid at his feet. He wished to claw out his eyes. He wished to rip out his own heart. The creature before him had once been the most beautiful of females in all the world, with hair that flowed like golden ribbons and eyes the color of the deepest ocean. She had been his everything. She had been his mate.

"Why? Why do you do this to us?" Segar wailed at the walls sweating with life-giving water. "Do not be a coward. Speak!"

"You and I both know the reason, merman," spoke the great voice of the island.

"We will not drink the water," he growled defiantly. "We will not bend to you. We prefer to die, leaving you to suffer a slow torturous death, infested by humans who will starve you with their greedy hearts."

It was what she deserved for having taken away their women, turning them into these ferocious sea creatures, these abominations of the night. For they had once been a beautiful people, like peacocks of the sea with flowing tails of every color and peace in their hearts. It was said they could control the sky above them and command the ocean around them, that they were loved by the Earth.

Captivated by the story, Liv planted herself on the floor with her legs crossed. She wondered if this was the retelling of something that had actually happened or a made-up story. And if real, then where had their power gone? Had the island taken it?

Now they were merely slaves—mad and weak.

The island's embittered laughter filled his ears. "Well, then, merman. I will continue to kill your mates. One by one. They will wash up on the shore so you may look upon their faces and be reminded of who truly holds all the power."

Segar had never been a man to hate. But he hated this place. He hated her—the island—with every fiber of his being. It was the reason he and his men had vowed to stop eating and stop drinking the sacred water that made them strong and live for hundreds of years.

"Why do you do this to us?" he said.

"Because you attempted to leave me unprotected," she spat. "And my survival is far more important than your need for sex or female companionship."

"They are our mates. They are everything to us." But she already knew that. It was why the island changed their women in the first place. It was why she made the sun poisonous to their skin and eyes—for where could they swim away to when the island's underwater caves were the only shelter from the sun for a thousand miles. The waters of this island had become their women's prison and, sea creatures or not, the men would never leave their mates.

"I have already met with the elders," Segar said, "and we have decided that if we cannot live as free men with our mates, we choose death."

Segar had already begun to feel the effects of not drinking the island's sacred water. His body felt tired and black spots had begun to appear on his skin. Death would come swiftly now. However, he was far too old to care and far too weary of seeing his people suffer. Now that his mate had died, he had no reason to go on.

Segar carefully lifted the creature with smooth black skin and long tendrils of dark seaweed-like hair and held her cold body tightly against his. "I'm sorry, my love, that I couldn't save you. But the island will pay for her sins. Someday, she will pay for the pain she's caused us all. I swear it."

He turned toward the jagged mouth of the cavern that led outside into the forest.

"Wait. Perhaps we can reach a compromise," said the voice of the island.

"Those are stories written about our deceased elders," said an oh-so-sensually masculine voice.

Liv's pulse spiked. "Jeez, you scared me." Or was her heart racing because Roen now stood in the room, his sensual scent filling the air?

Definitely Roen, she thought while her chest tightened along with every erogenous zone in her body.

Liv looked up to find six and half or so feet of endless ropes of glistening, bronzed muscles on full display in his usual distracting "nothing of an outfit"—a strip of suede around his lower torso, long enough to reach mid-thigh. She really wished he'd start wearing clothing that didn't make her want to light some candles, sacrifice a helpless creature, and throw herself at his feet every time he entered a room.

Uh, you feel the same way when he's in a suit, Liv.

Then there was her heart. It fluttered and danced with joy every time she thought of him. *Don't, Liv. He doesn't love you back. He doesn't want this.*

She instantly felt her mood sour.

"There are more translated texts," he said, "in the next aisle over." He flicked his thumb to his right and then held out his large, inviting hand to help her up. She stared at it for a moment, remembering how warm it was and the things it had done to her body.

Come on, Liv. Don't torture yourself.

She closed the book in her hands with a loud *thwap!* and popped from the floor on her own. "Will any of them explain why you insist on wearing such skimpy clothes?"

He dropped his hand, his eyes noting the rejection, while his mouth formed a teasingly sensual smile. "To tempt the ladies, of course. Glad to see my strategy is working."

She arched an irritated brow.

He shrugged those broad, naked, smooth shoulders. "Sounded more appealing than the truth—we live here alone most of the time and considering our tolerance to the cold, we don't need clothes."

"Are you trying to say you all hate doing laundry?"

"Exactly."

"We wear these," he looked down at his suede, "burn them, and order more when we run out."

That was so manlike. "Then why not go around naked?"

"We're not savages, Liv."

Again, she threw a raised brow his way.

"All right. Perhaps we are. However, full nudity is reserved for fighting. Or sex. But usually fighting since most of us prefer women and there aren't many of those around here."

"So showing your penis is equivalent to throwing down the gauntlet. Does size come into play?" She had to ask.

"Are you asking if we're intimidated if the other man has a larger penis?"

She nodded.

"You must think us shallow."

Yep.

"Fine," he said. "Yes. A larger penis may create doubt in the opponent's mind." He shrugged. "What can I say? We are men. Mermen."

And there wasn't a woman on the planet who wouldn't feel somewhat intimidated or awed in their presence because of that.

"What about the red, black, and suede?" she asked.

"A tradition handed down for many generations. Animal skin was harder to come by due to the lack of animal life here—I think our early ancestors ate them all. So only the leader and elders were allowed to wear it. Red signifies those who have yet to find mates, and black means they have found someone."

Liv covered her mouth in horror. "Oh God." All of the men she'd seen who wore black sarongs had women who'd been turned into creatures.

"They wear the black in honor of their mates," he added.

Liv imagined it was symbolic of death and of mourning.

"Are the colors they wear any indicator of who's going to side with you?" The moment the question sprang from her lips, she remembered that Shane wore black and he didn't side with Roen on anything.

"No. This is why the meeting with the elders took so long."

"What was the outcome?" she asked, hesitant to hear any more bad news.

"They are all familiar with the scriptures—" he flicked his thumb to the aisle to his left this time "—and everyone agrees that the wheels are in motion as predicted with only two possible outcomes."

Liv remembered two of the men discussing some sort of prophecy triggered by Roen's arrival. They didn't seem aligned, however, on which outcome would prevail. Their healer Holden, a Harvard graduate and doctor, believed if the men stuck together, they'd be freed and their mates would be brought back. Jason believed it signified the beginning of the end.

Liv shook her head. "What do you believe?"

"That our next move must be thought out carefully and war among us should be avoided at all costs. We can only win this if we remain united. I also think that being in the same room with you is driving me *foking* mad."

He stepped in close and wrapped his strong arm around her waist, holding her to him. She gazed up into those shimmering green eyes filled with lust, knowing she should push him away after everything he'd said, but that wasn't going to happen. Her lips craved his kiss, like her heart craved his love.

Slowly, he lowered his mouth to hers, and the restrained kiss immediately sent steamy shockwaves through her body. She slid her arms to his broad shoulders, her hands taking their time to caress every bulging ripple on the way up. Meanwhile, his hot tongue glided between her lips and stroked her in the most sinful manner, each movement—a push forward and slow pull back—mimicking what their bodies wanted.

The entire room filled with that strange buzzing sensation, and she leaned into him, letting the warmth and spicy smell of his body envelop her senses. Everything about Roen felt so right, so good, so irresistible. She just couldn't help feeling lost in him and wanting more. So much more.

Roen effortlessly lifted her by the waist, and she wrapped her legs around him, hiking up her dress in the process. He carried her back toward the sitting area, their mouths locked together in a fiery mess, their surroundings melting away. They could be anywhere right now, and it wouldn't change a thing. They could only see and hear and feel each other.

Roen slowly lowered Liv onto the soft brown couch in front of the fireplace, leaving her sitting up so he could kneel between her bare legs—bare everything. She wore no undergarments, leaving her completely exposed to him.

He broke away from her mouth and slid his hot tongue down the length of her neck, stopping at the base to suck the sensitive skin. She threaded her fingers into his soft, caramel brown hair, and his hand moved to her breast, softly kneading and cupping the tender mound, instantly making the nipple pucker into a tight little bead.

When Roen's sinful mouth moved to that delicious spot between her shoulder and neck, she felt him scrape his teeth against the skin. Liv instinctually froze. Roen had bit her hard once in the throes of passion. He'd said he couldn't help himself. This time, however, Roen bit down softly, like any man might, and the sensation was too sensual to make him stop.

His warm, rough hand slowly slid down her body, making its way to her inner thigh, where the tips of his thick fingers made tiny strokes, back and forth, over the sensitive skin just centimeters from her hot slick entrance.

What was he trying to do to her?

She nudged her hips toward his teasing hand in a silent plea to end the torture, but he denied the contact she hungered for, pulling his hand slightly back.

She let out a helpless little whimper and rubbed the inside of her right knee and thigh against his hip. "What are you waiting for, Roen?" She panted her words.

His biting, licking mouth broke away from her neck. "I don't want to hurt you. You need to be ready for me," he said in a husky low voice, his hot breath tickling her skin as he spoke.

"I'm ready," she panted. "I'm ready."

He pulled away, placing his free hand on her cheek, his thumb pushing and rubbing her lower lip while he stared into her eyes with an animalistic hunger. "I'll be the judge of that." He moved his other thumb to her entrance, circling and teasing, before sliding it up and down, spreading her wetness over the delicate, tingling flesh.

Oh, God. Her breath caught in her throat.

"You like that, don't you, Liv? You like it when I touch you." He possessively watched her wordless reply—her accelerated breathing, her eyes, her parted wet lips—as he expertly teased the tiny bundle of nerves ready to explode.

"Yes." She threw back her head, unable to stand the torture any further.

"I'm the only man who can make you feel this good. Because you're mine, Liv. Don't ever forget that." He then sharply thrust his thick fingers into her, and when her head snapped down, he smothered her gasp with a hot, demanding kiss. With each hard push of his fingers, his thumb continued working her throbbing bud while his tongue and mouth drank in her escalating cries of pleasure.

By now, he had to realize she was ready. She had been from the moment he'd entered the room. She always felt ready for him. Always.

"Damn, you're so wet," he said between searing hot kisses, "and ready for me."

Their tongues continued dancing wildly together, as if they couldn't get enough of each other's taste and touch; meanwhile their bodies moved in a wild sexual rhythm.

What's he waiting for? Oh God, I need him. She reached for his sides, trying to pull the two of them together, burning for more than just his fingers. She wanted to feel the girth of his silky, rock-hard shaft working into her, answering the call of every erotic pulse and throb deep inside her with his thrusting, pounding cock. She wanted to feel his velvety moist head buried deep, pushing against her until it hurt, until he could go no further. She wanted to experience the delicious twitching of his hard flesh releasing his cum inside her walls. The animalistic need burned through her, consuming any rational thoughts with its raging fire.

"Please, Roen. Fuck me," she said. "I'm begging you." He answered her request by removing his fingers, gripping her firmly by the hips, and pulling her sharply forward on the couch, positioning the wet, heated juncture between her legs exactly where he needed.

He once again sucked and licked his way down her neck and gently bit while grinding his erection against her, denying her body what it agonized for.

"Is this what you want?" His voice was gruff and filled with the promise of hard, hot fucking if she simply pleased him with the right words.

Did he want her to beg? Because she would. "Please. Whatever you want, you can have it."

"That's good. Because my kind can go all night, and I plan to fuck you until you're weak and raw and can't take anymore. And then you'll thank me by sucking my cock until I've spilled every last drop of cum left in my body." He reached for the knot at his waist. "Now, open your legs nice and wide for me."

His raw, explicit words sparked erotic images in her mind of the two of them wringing every last ounce of pleasure from each other's bodies. It nearly sent her over the edge.

She did as she was told, spreading her thighs, her most intimate flesh opened to him, ready to accept anything he could dish out. Just as long as he gave her what she needed and ended her agony. Her body felt like it was covered in firecracker fuses, each one lit, spitting out sparks of torturous yearning, but failing to make it home to deliver that grand explosion.

Ohmygod. This is insane. If his touches and kisses alone could make her feel this sinfully tormented, she could only imagine the ecstasy of having him inside her. And it all felt so different from before, a thousand times more powerful than when they'd almost been together. It was like her love for him had only fueled her physical attraction. But did he know? Did he understand that this was so much more than simple lust? And that her body only responded to him like this because he'd won her heart?

"Roen, I…" When she pulled her mouth away, she suddenly noticed how his half-mast gaze also held something more. Yes, something had changed in Roen's temperament, too. She then realized he hadn't been mauling her with his insatiable lust, like before. He hadn't been trying to tear away her clothes in order to fuck like ravenous animals. His touch was still passionate and everything dominating she knew a man like him had to be, but he'd been holding back, making sure this moment wasn't wasted or ruined by his primal desires.

"Are you all right?" he asked.

She nodded, too overrun with emotions to speak.

"Good. Because I don't want you to have any regrets, Liv. Not when it comes to me."

Tears welled in her eyes. *Oh God. I love him so much. I can't do this. I can't.* She couldn't keep going when it would only make her love him more.

"Roen, I don't want this."

"I won't hurt you. I can control my urges. Except one. I need you. I need to be inside you."

She shook her head from side to side. "It's not enough, Roen." She maneuvered around his kneeling body to stand. She wouldn't be able to say what was in her heart with their skin touching. "I love you. And I know you think it's not real or some effect of being mates, but I know I love you. If we sleep together, I won't be able to let go."

His head fell forward, and he ran his hands through his mussed hair. "I don't think this confrontation will end well. I feel it in my gut." She knew he referred to the brewing fight.

So the man who never fails is afraid of failing.

"I think that's fear talking," she said. "And I think it's why you'll succeed. Because you will do anything in your power to not fail. It terrifies you too much."

He slowly rose from the floor and took a seat on the couch. "I'm glad you're so confident, but I'm not, which is why I decided I need this. You. Me. Once. I don't want to leave this world not knowing what it's like to be with my mate or without giving her the pleasure only I can provide. We need this, Liv. I need this. I realized it the moment I thought you were dead, eaten alive by the maids. All I could think of was how I would've given anything for one more day with you."

He hadn't gone as far as saying he loved her, and it didn't matter. She felt his love, and every little cell in her heart swelled up with sadness. She too wanted this, but… "It's not enough, Roen. I want you. All of you. Not just one night or even one week. I want you. And I think—no—I know you're going to push me away again, and it will break me, Roen."

"I think you're stronger than you give yourself credit for."

He really didn't understand what she'd gone through when they'd separated the first time. Or, perhaps he did. How the hell would she know? He had never truly opened up. Either way, after several months of feeling like her heart might dislodge from her chest every time it took a beat, she eventually got to a point where she could function again and start thinking about important things like going back to school. But make no mistake, life felt different. She felt broken inside. Living had lost its meaning, and the best she could hope for would be going through the motions and faking her way through every breath.

"What I had after leaving you wasn't living, Roen. It was surviving. And there is no doubt in my mind that the moment you're able, you'll send me away, claiming that you're saving me when you're really saving yourself."

"I'm not worried about myself—that's ridiculous," he replied.

"Then tell me what's really going on inside that head of yours. Say the truth—hard, cold, and ugly. I think we owe each other that much."

"Are you sure? The truth isn't always pleasant."

"Yes," she clasped her hands together and lifted her chin, "tell me honestly why you keep pushing me away."

"Because, despite wishing things were different, I will never be able to give you what you need: to come first."

"Roen Doran is a man who finds a way to get what he wants despite the odds. Why don't you believe we'll figure something out?"

He looked up at her, mildly irritated. Or frustrated. Or exasperated, like she was. "Why do you continually doubt that I've thought this through? I watched my parents try to form some semblance of a normal life, and it destroyed my mother. I finally know it's because the island always came first. Not her heart, not his children. *This* island. Worse, he put us in danger, and when my mother took us away to protect us, it drove them both mad. Not only because of the separation, but because deep down inside, they probably knew he'd failed us." Roen looked up at Liv with deep pain in his eyes. "They loved each other. It didn't work. It won't work for us."

"We're not them, Roen. We're not—"

"Liv, I want you more than anything. But what will such selfishness accomplish? Only pain in the end, because I cannot ignore the facts. Somehow my mother avoided becoming a maid. I have no doubt it was because my father made a deal with the island, and I have no doubt in my mind that my mother, Lyle, and I were used to make him obey, including murdering innocent people. Do you honestly believe for one second that I would want that to be our life? Or our children's? Because it will be." He sighed bitterly. "I cannot separate myself from this place. I will never be free of her, but I'll die making sure you are."

Liv stood there for a moment, feeling her heart pound away in her chest, urging her to reason with Roen and make him understand that they might find a way. Only, she could easily see their story playing out in an identical tragedy. More importantly, she couldn't stand to see the torment in his eyes—torment over what might happen to her because of him.

So what's the right thing to do? For him and for me?

The answer wasn't very pretty.

She sat down beside him and placed her hand over his. "I'll help you, then," she said glumly. "I'll read through the texts and find out what I can about how the mermaids are transformed, and I'll help you find a way to break our bond."

He flashed a weak smile. "I thought mates only went crazy after they were separated."

She shrugged, trying to bring the conversation to a less depressing place. "We're both mature adults. We've both come to the conclusion that we can't be together under the circumstances. So, why not try to find a way to help each other and help ourselves?"

"I thought you believed our feelings were irreversible," he said skeptically.

"Maybe I'm wrong. Wouldn't be the first time. But I know if I really love you, I'll do what's right, even if my heart's not in it. Just as long as you're sure this is what you want."

"Yes. I mean no." He rubbed his face. "I only know I don't want to ever put you in harm's way, and this place—my world isn't safe for you. I'm not safe for you."

No. Probably not. She might get turned into a monster or squashed by the island, who didn't want landlovers around. What had Roen said? They were like a virus.

She popped from the couch and clapped her hands together, masking her devastation and wanting to keep a stiff upper lip—he had enough to worry about already. "So let's rip off the Band-Aid and get to work."

Roen rose from the couch, and Liv couldn't help notice his semi-aroused state.

He noted where her eyes locked. "Sorry." He shrugged. "I can't help it. I still want you."

"I know how you feel—think I'm going to go take a cold shower now."

Roen made a small laugh, and it warmed her heart. Everything about him did. "I was thinking the same."

Triple X images of the two of them showering together exploded in her mind. "I'll go back to the cottages," she said hurriedly, needing to get the hell out of there.

"No. It isn't safe. The situation is delicate and fighting could break out at any moment. There's a shower down here. You use one of the bathrooms upstairs."

"Okay. Good plan." She bolted from the room.

CHAPTER TWELVE

After a long, cold shower to shock her body back into a semi-coherent state, Liv had gone to check on Dana, who still slept peacefully in one of the spacious guest rooms. It had been a trying few days, and the fun was only getting started. Liv could feel the ominous, angry energy in the air every time she took a breath. Even the hair on the back of her neck knew that this latest episode with the cruise ship was only the beginning. A damned frightening thought. Liv had never seen anything so horrifying—blood and bodies filling the harbor.

Those poor, poor women. And poor them because whatever came next, it couldn't be good. Which is why Liv wanted Dana away from there as badly as Roen wanted Liv gone.

How the hell are we ever going to get off this damned rock?

Liv's thoughts returned to the conversation with Roen about the island having limits to her abilities and how the camouflage truly worked. The point being that an underlying physical connection or chemistry was used to make everything happen. The island was not a witch with magical powers. She was an expert at smoke and mirrors. A master of illusions.

And deception.

What was Crazy Dirt trying to hide with all of these rituals and rules and displays of power? *What does anyone who wants to stay in power try to hide? Their weakness.*

So it stood to reason that every action Crazy Dirt took, every threat she made, only served to cloud the truth. A truth that might help them figure out how she pulled the strings—to create the maids, control the men, and reach across the ocean into someone's head.

Liv quickly dressed, throwing back on her long black stretchy dress and black leather sandals. She wrapped her long dark hair into a ponytail and scurried downstairs back to the library, carefully checking the hallway to ensure she did not bump into Roen in his towel. Seeing Roen wet and fresh from a shower would end her thinking for the day.

With the coast clear, Liv entered the library slash aquarium, her brain tingling with excitement, knowing she was onto something. It was like the time she'd run a study at the university, monitoring the brainwaves of people when shown pictures of people they knew. Family, friends, and spouses—the brain would light up in a very special way when it saw a face the subject loved. This was nothing new in the scientific world, though it sparked an idea.

Liv then placed couples in two separate rooms and hooked them up to brainwave monitors. She then showed one of the subjects pictures of people they loved—mother, friend, brother, child, and finally their significant other. The brain lit up with each image; however, when the subject thought of the person in the other room, who stared at a white wall, that person's brain showed a small flicker of light. That's right. The subject staring at the wall showed activity when their significant other thought about them. All the way from the other goddamned room. Miraculous. It led her to believe that emotional bonds between people—love being the strongest—were physical, too.

"Liv? What are you doing?" Dana's groggy voice came from the other end of the long room. She wore the same black dress and had her long brown hair in a braid down one side.

"I'm standing here spinning inside my head. How are you feeling?"

Dana slogged her way over. "My arms still hurts a little, but at least I'm alive—something I can't say for Cindy or those poor other women." Dana stopped a few feet from Liv and wrapped her arms around her stomach.

Liv gave Dana's shoulder a squeeze. "I know, honey. I know. But I promise, Roen will find a way to get us home."

Dana's eyes widened. "I don't want to go home. I want to see Shane."

Not this again. And changing subjects... "Do you remember my thesis paper?"

Dana rolled her eyes. "You mean the one where people's brains are like giant radio antennas and we go through life trying to home in on our 'one true love'? You mean that one?"

Liv grumbled disapprovingly. That had only been a part of her theory meant to explain how people who'd never met fell instantly in love. "I'm talking about the piece related to love and connections between people happening on a physical level we can't see or measure."

"Oh. That," Dana said dryly.

"You laugh, but it's real. And obviously the people here have evolved with a stronger connection. Maybe they even have some sort of heightened ability to tap into each other or humans or I don't know." She only knew that Roen, his people, and their home had their own distinct evolutionary and biological story. The fact they only produced male offspring was proof of that.

"I didn't laugh," Dana pointed out.

Liv shot her a look.

"Jeez. Just kidding." Dana held up her palms. "What's your point?"

"I'm not sure yet. I feel like I'm missing something. Something big that could help Roen and those men." Liv placed her hand on her hip, staring at the thousands of books. It might take years to find patterns and uncover what made this island tick. Didn't they have a computer for cross-referencing information?

She'd have to go see Roen. The thought made her heart speed up and her body heat. She wondered if at that very moment Roen found himself becoming inexplicably aroused because of their bond. She laughed. Wouldn't that be convenient if they were a couple? *Liv to Roen. Liv to Roen. Wake up your penis, I'm coming to bed now.*

Liv shook off her ridiculous thought. "Dana, I have to go find Roen." She jerked her head for Dana to follow.

"I'm going to head back upstairs and take a shower."

Liv eyed Dana suspiciously. "You promise you're not going to leave this house?"

"Why would I?" Dana said. "There are monsters out there."

"Because you're still under the delusion that you want to be claimed by a merman?"

"I won't leave. I promise." Dana held up her right palm.

"I'll be right back." Liv went out into the hallway and immediately found a "red skirt" with a tattoo of an enormous sea serpent covering half his body. The man had long black dreads, huge arms, and looked like he ate people for breakfast.

Liv straightened her spine. She needed to get used to not feeling intimidated by these huge men.

"Where's Roen? I need to talk to him," she said.

The goliath man frowned at her and opened his mouth, surely to deliver some macho-merman gibberish meant to demoralize her.

I don't have time for this. "Eh!" She pointed her finger in his face. "Don't you dare start. Tell me where Roen is, or so help me fish gods, I will find a way to turn your gonads into tiny caviar unfit for a gas station sushi roll."

The man flashed her a concerned look, clearly pondering if fighting her would be a better option versus bothering Roen.

"I'm in a hurry, if you haven't noticed," she added.

The man pointed toward the dining room, which led to the kitchen. "Through the kitchen, take a right. You'll see a short passageway and stairwell leading down."

"Thank you." Liv went on her way, grinning proudly until she reached that dark stairwell with stone steps and a closed door at the bottom. It looked like it led to a damned dungeon.

Don't be such a wuss. It's not like he keeps mermaids down there.

She descended and pushed open the door. "Roen, I need to know where…" Liv noticed Roen and five old men seated around a dark, circular, wooden table. Each man had long white hair and a beard and looked suspiciously similar to the life-sized oil paintings of the fierce men—carrying spears, machetes, or swords—on the walls behind them. It was like looking at an exhibit of before and afters.

"Liv, what is the meaning of this?" Roen snarled, standing from the table.

She held out her palms. "I'm so sorry. Really. But I need the data you've been collecting on the island."

Roen made a rumble deep in his chest and stormed toward her, grabbing her elbow and dragging her back up the stairs.

"Out!" Roen barked at a few men prepping food in the modern, industrial chef's kitchen. "And you!" he yelled at Liv. "What is the meaning of this? You cannot interrupt a meeting with the elders like that; they could have you executed."

Liv lowered one corner of her mouth. "This is important."

Roen crossed his arms over his bare chest. "You have five seconds."

"Love. We're missing love."

Roen groaned and dug the heel of his palm into his forehead. "Liv, I thought we settled this—"

"No! Not us. I'm talking about the island. Love, reproduction, bonds—it's what drives the underlying habits and behaviors of every species. And the more evolved the species, the more complex and sophisticated the bonds between them."

"What's your point, Liv?" Roen asked exasperatedly.

She couldn't say the truth and risk the island realizing what she was really after: finding the island's weakness so maybe they could turn the table on their situation. To do that, she needed to understand what made Crazy Dirt tick.

"I'm not sure yet," Liv replied. "I need to see that data."

"It's stored over in the science center."

"You have a science center?" Liv furrowed her brows.

He shrugged. "Of course. Why wouldn't we?"

"Ohmygod." Liv pinched the bridge of her nose and shook her head. "This place is so bizarre."

"I can tell you, however, the data they collect is related to temperature, water properties, air quality, and level of contaminants in the surrounding ocean. All meant to assist us in creating an artificial habitat if necessary."

"Your plan B is moving an entire island?"

"No. Building an enclosed, secured structure around her."

Liv raised her brows. "Like I said: bizarre. Well, maybe I should take a look anyway. It could help me understand more about her as an organism."

"The project is in its infancy, I'm afraid, so they won't be able to tell you much. Right now they're focused on understanding life-support elements—the basics to sustain her."

"You mean her food source?" And did he have any clue how speaking with him like this was turning her on? *God, I love science. So. Hot.* Almost as hot as anthropology and sociology.

"She doesn't eat. But yes, more or less." Roen glanced back at the stairwell. "Liv, I respect your desire to help us, but—"

"But what, Roen? I'm a landlover and couldn't possibly have the intellect to be of any use or understand?" She narrowed her eyes.

Roen clenched his jaw, and she watched the little muscles pulse with tension. "*But* I must go now. The elders say I must release Shane. He's broken no laws and—"

A man burst into the kitchen. "Roen!"

Roen rolled his eyes, likely on his last inch of patience. "What now?"

"There's smoke coming from the mountain."

"Smoke?" Roen asked.

"Why smoke?" Liv asked.

"It's probably you-know-who letting off steam. Nothing to worry about." Roen pointed in Liv's face. "You stay here, Liv. I mean it. Do not leave this house." He turned and rushed from the room.

Yeah, that's totally how I act when it's 'nothing to worry about.'

Suddenly, Liv felt a frigid wave of doom wash over her, like a tidal wave straight from an icy hell. Something bad was coming. Something big and ugly that would separate her and Roen forever. *What the hell was that?* The feeling was so strong, it almost pushed her over. She hoped those were nerves talking, and not the island subliminally declaring war.

"Be careful, Ro…" He was already gone.

CHAPTER THIRTEEN

Cold rain drizzled from the dark gray sky, casting a gloomy shadow over the path that led from Roen's home to the great hall situated in the heart of the mountain. He had no idea what awaited, but he hoped it was nothing more than what he'd told Liv: the island blowing off some steam. He knew she was upset—everyone knew—but sonofabitch, what had the island been thinking?

Seeing those women torn apart this morning had left an indelible mark on his soul, only fueling his conviction that this way of life had to cease. Then there'd been that moment when he'd believed Liv among the dead, and he'd felt his world crumble. Without her somewhere in his life, he had a difficult time seeing a path forward.

The mountain in the center of the island rumbled and a plume of oily black smoke erupted from its snowcapped peak.

What the foke was that?

He'd never seen the mountain smoke, and they used the great hall frequently—for claimings, dispute resolution, issuing the men's weekly rations of sacred water, and celebrations—though they didn't have many of those. Life on the island was mainly dedicated to working—building, standing guard, fishing, upkeep of equipment and boats, or keeping the grounds. A small, very specialized group studied the island for the project he mentioned to Liv.

Of course, I left out a few things. He saw no point discussing how the island's health had been deteriorating for years—water production declining and her behavior becoming more erratic, sometimes going silent for years as if sleeping or trying to conserve energy. They assumed the massive pollution of the oceans and global warming might be to blame, which was why Roen initiated the project. He'd be damned if he followed in his father's footsteps, blowing up factories or sinking ships. Murder was not the solution. Mankind either evolved into a more conscientious species or the planet would perish.

That is if you don't foke things up for everyone first. Roen now feared he would be the cause of all life ending. If he failed to persuade the island to adapt to modern ways and failed at freeing his people, it would all be over. *Change isn't inevitable; it's necessary for survival.*

Roen reached the jagged mouth of the great hall and paused outside. The sound of screaming—not the violent sort, but the suffering sort—echoed outside. He immediately tensed, his mind going into a state of hyperalertness. He grabbed a fallen branch from a pine tree situated next to the entrance and entered, ready for anything.

"Anything except this," he muttered under his breath, taking in the horrific and chaotic scene before him.

Some of the men clawed at the walls of the cavern, their fingertips raw and bloody. Others held pickaxes and pounded away at the empty pool. Some lay on the slate-gray stone floor, pressing the heels of their palms to their temples or eyes, moaning in agony.

Holden, their healer, lay closest to Roen, writhing on the floor in pain, his mop of curly red hair flopping from side to side. Roen kneeled down and gripped Holden's shoulder. "Holden, can you hear me?"

Holden, who looked like his face had been sunburned, groaned in agony, covering his face.

"Holden, if you can hear me, tell me what's happening."

"It burns. It burns."

"What burns?" Roen asked.

"My eyes."

Roen pulled Holden's hands from his face. "Open your eyes. Let me see," Roen commanded.

"No. I can't. It burns too much," the man wailed. "I need the water. I need the water."

Roen pried the man's right lid open, catching a glimpse of what was inside. "Foking hell." Roen snapped his hand away. Holden's eyes were blood red.

The man who'd come to retrieve him, a fellow with sandy-blond hair, was in the corner, giving another man sips from a bottle of water.

Roen rushed over. "What are you doing?"

The blond man moved to help another. "It's my water ration."

"Is it helping them?" Roen asked.

"Yes, sir, but I don't have enough."

Roen looked over his shoulder at the man who'd received a small sip. He got right up and his eyes appeared normal. "You! Tell me what happened," Roen commanded.

He rubbed his red face and then ran his hands through his short dark hair. "I don't know, sir. I was outside working and my skin and eyes started burning. I ran straight here, but there's no more water."

A punishment. Roen knew the island would lash out, though who could've anticipated this? He'd expected her to come after him.

"You two," Roen pointed to the two men who'd been healed, "go through everyone's homes and round up all of the rations. Bring them back here."

The two men hesitated. There were very strict rules about entering another man's home—one of the many quirks of being a merman. Each man was granted a piece of land on the island, and no one could enter uninvited with a few exceptions. A home was a merman's castle, which he built with his own two hands, which was why the men who were handy with a hammer had the better homes. Obviously the rule didn't apply to the leader.

"I'm giving you permission," Roen said. "No. I'm ordering you."

"Yes, sir." The two men nodded and ran off.

"The question you should be asking yourself right now, merman," said that chilling female voice, *"is where this will end?"*

He knew she'd eventually pop up for air. "We're not backing down. You can't threaten your way out of this."

"Who said anything about threats?" she chuckled her words. *"I'm going to wipe you all from the face of this earth."*

"And risk being unprotected? I don't think that's wise. Not when I'm offering you another solution—protection from the world we live in today. It's only a question of time before humans discover us."

"You think I need protection from humans, Roen? Because I'll strike them first. In a few days, they're going to begin noticing what happens when my mermen step out of line—imagine entire cities going mad, people clawing out their eyes, suffocating in the streets. They'll think it's biological warfare, and what will happen then, Roen? How many wars will start when they lash out at their enemies?"

Absorbed in his conversation with the island, Roen had almost forgotten where he was: standing in the middle of a room of screaming mermen who never so much as flinched when in pain. That's when he noticed one poor man had taken his machete and sliced his own throat. Blood pooled on the floor around him.

"No. Goddammit, no," Roen said, shocked, stunned, and angry as hell.

"Oh no. Something wrong, merman? A little blood gotcha scared? Because just you wait. They'll all be dead by morning, driven mad by the pain, and then I'll get started on the landlovers."

He fisted his hands, wishing he could kill her. "What do you want?" he growled.

She cackled triumphantly. *"Ah. Well, I'm not sure yet. So let's start with an offering of good faith to get started. I'll take your mate."*

"You can't have Liv," he snarled.

"That's my price to stop this madness from spreading. I want Liv. Of course, that will be your first punishment for turning the men against me. One of many."

Roen's fear for his people closed in on him—had he made a mistake? Then he remembered his dream. The one where the island kept pushing him to choose between saving Liv or saving his men. *This is what she always does.* And probably was the same method of control used with his father.

Then, those childhood memories—nightmares, really—flooded his thoughts. Those boys in the group home, where he'd lived after his mother died, beat him every day. They broke his nose, they kicked his balls so many times he'd coughed up blood for weeks. No one lifted a finger to stop them, and it was the moment he realized it was up to him. No one was coming to save him. And they weren't going to stop, because they enjoyed it too much. When the next violent confrontation happened, he was ready. He fought back with a goddamned baseball bat that delivered one broken arm and a concussion. Not nearly sufficient payback, but they never touched him again. From then on he knew those who didn't stand up to bullies were only inviting them back for more.

Don't back down. Don't ever back down. Because godfokingdammit this had to end.

"You're trying to make me choose between Liv and everyone else, and I won't. We want changes. We want the women back like you promised. So until you're ready to be reasonable, this conversation is over."

Silence.

Roen didn't mistake it for a victory. This was far, far from over, and he could only hope his move wasn't the wrong choice. It was one thing to go down fighting, but it was another to take everyone down with him.

After Roen left, Liv ran upstairs to warn Dana about something bad going down, only to discover an empty room.

Her temper shot off like a bottle rocket, quickly fizzling into terror. "No. No. No." Liv checked ten of the bedrooms, the library, the kitchen, and a few other places. No Dana.

Shane. It was the only other place Liv could think of. Dana had some sort of attraction to that despicable man—okay, Dana liked them all—and she seemed to like Shane the most. Thank God he'd already found a mate, as indicated by the black cloth he wore.

So where was the prison? Liv went to ask one of the men, but everyone had disappeared.

Liv ran out the front door, screaming for Dana, and crashed straight into Roen's hard, bare chest.

With her hands firmly on his pectorals, she shook her head, trying to remain focused. "Dana is gone."

Roen growled. "I told you to stay inside the house. Don't your damned ears work, woman?"

Liv felt her nostrils flare with outrage. "I'm going to pretend, merman, that I didn't just hear you say that."

"Why do you say merman like it was an insult?"

"Why do you say woman like it was an insult?" she barked back. "Wait. You know what? I don't have time for this. Where's Shane?"

"Why do you ask?"

"Because," she replied hastily, "I think that's where Dana went. She's got some sort of thing for him—okay? I don't know why."

Roen frowned, his face flushed. "I cannot deal with this right now." He pushed past her, then stopped and reached for her wrist. "You're coming back inside."

"No. I'm not!" She jerked back her hand. *Damn, he has a grip.*

"Liv, the island is doing something to the men. I need to return to the great hall. You also need to stay away from me. Far away—please go into one of the guest rooms."

"What kind of something? And why do I need to stay away?"

Roen walked faster than she could keep up. Those big long, muscle-packed legs were much more agile than they appeared. "I'm not sure yet. Their eyes burn. As for staying away, I'm not in control. Not even a little bit and your smell is driving me mad, woman."

Liv tripped, but caught herself. "Is the island doing it? And I don't know what to do about my smell. I'm sorry." Why were they having these two very different conversations at the same time?

"Maybe—I don't know." Roen stormed up the staircase, taking them two at a time. "Go into the guest room and lock the door—the need for you is killing me."

Liv was not about to hide from Roen. He was the one person she knew would never harm her.

"How is she doing it?" Liv panted, only halfway up the staircase. Because if it could happen to them, it might happen to Roen, too.

"That doesn't matter. Getting her to stop does," he called out from somewhere upstairs.

Liv followed the sound of his voice. "You can't give in, Roen." She walked past the guest rooms, turned down a long corridor with gleaming black tile floors, and stopped in the doorway, her heart doing a little flutter. *Oh my.* The room was enormous with a large stone fireplace and velvety furniture upholstered in rich dark reds and browns. The flooring, made of dark stained wood, made the room feel intimate and cozy, just perfect for shutting out the world. *Or making love all day long.*

"This is your bedroom?" she asked.

"Yes."

She'd only seen the guest rooms and that included the night she'd spent with Roen when he'd resisted completing the Claiming Ceremony.

"It's, um…nice." She gulped.

He had an extra-large, four-post bed with a giant mural on the ceiling of a lonely mermaid perched on a rock, looking out over a wide ocean toward an island off in the distance. The silhouette of a man stared back at her, and the longing in the maid's eyes told a story of utter loneliness. Imagining Roen falling asleep each night looking up at that mural broke her heart. Imagining Roen in this big empty bed by himself felt even worse.

"Liv?" Roen snapped his fingers.

When she looked up at Roen, who now held two corked glass bottles in his hands, she knew he'd caught on to what she'd been thinking. His eyes moved several times between the bed and her face. Then the bed and her breasts. She saw the unmistakable sign of his semi-arousal pushing out his suede, followed by the air filling with that strange vibration, signaling he wanted her as badly as she wanted him.

Liv closed her eyes and took a deep breath, telling her body to stand down. *Especially you, nipples.* No doubt, they were poking out through her black dress.

When she opened her eyes again, the look of pain and despair on Roen's face broke the camel's back. *This is ridiculous.* She couldn't take him lying alone every night when she loved him so much it hurt.

And now that horrifying, ominous feeling in her gut told her something bad was coming. Something that would separate them permanently.

God, she wanted to tell him, but how the hell would that help anyone? By making him paranoid or triggering a self-fulfilling prophecy?

Surprisingly, all her earlier apprehensions about being with him vanished, and she completely understood what he'd been trying to say earlier. There wasn't going to be a tomorrow or later. This was it for them. How, she didn't know. But God help her, she couldn't bear the thought of never knowing, or worse, deprive him of that memory if she were the one who didn't survive.

"This is torture, Liv. And I really can't handle it right now—I've got to go." Roen headed for the door.

Liv sucked back her heavy thoughts. "I changed my mind. I want to sleep with you," she blurted out.

"What?" Roen halted halfway out the door.

She held up her chin. *You're a grown woman, Liv. And you want him. And you sure as hell won't live with yourself knowing you never gave this man what he wanted, too.*

"I want you to make love to me right there in that big bed." She wanted to show him with her entire body how much she loved him. "And after that," she said evenly, "I want you to fuck me hard like a goddamned animal." Because that was her other fantasy, and if this was it, she wanted both flavors of Roen. His soft and sweet side and rough and mermanly side.

Roen's big green eyes were wide while he gulped. "Now? Because, dammit, Liv, I really have to—"

"No. Of course not now. But as soon as you take care of your men and we find Dana, it's on."

He looked at her suspiciously. "What made you change your mind so quickly?"

She couldn't tell the truth: That she feared something terrible was coming and this was their last chance to be together. "I can't function like this. I practically orgasm every time I'm in the same room with you and not getting any release is driving me mad. I mean, seriously. Roen, if being apart was bad, this is worse." That had sounded convincing, right?

Roen stood there staring at her. "You want me to fuck you," he said, his voice filled with disbelief.

"Yeah. Well, make love first. Then fuck—wait. You're not going to throw out another excuse, are you? Because—"

"No!" He pushed out his hand. "I only wanted to make sure I heard you correctly. I'm in. And now I'm going to be as hard as a rock until I have you. Not that I'm complaining—neverthefokemind—I need to take care of this—" he held up the bottles "—and then see our elders to discuss the terms we will offer to the island."

"What? Roen, no. Don't throw in the towel. You've gotten this far, and your men are behind you."

"I am not throwing in the towel," he said. "But we must attempt to reason with her quickly before things get out of hand."

Yeah. Good luck with that. She sure as hell admired his optimism. He never quit.

"I'm going to go find Dana," she said. "I'll meet you back here."

Roen growled. "You need to stay. It isn't safe for you to be running around alone, especially when the maids are no longer deterred by daylight."

"I need to find my sister—like you said, it's not safe." She stepped in closer, narrowing her eyes.

"Fine. Come with me. We'll drop off the water in the great hall, and I'll take you down into the prison. It's near there."

Smart man.

CHAPTER FOURTEEN

It wasn't at all what Liv expected, although now she understood why Roen was freaking the hell out.

"I've never seen so much blood," she whispered, shocked with horror. And she'd never seen anyone claw at their own face. She covered her mouth, holding back the bile while her mind scrambled, unsure of what to do or how to help.

The unaffected men—about half of those in the room—quickly moved from victim to victim, pouring water into screaming mouths.

Okay, okay. I can do that.

She stepped forward, but Roen pulled her back. "No. You'll only get hurt, and we have plenty of help now." Roen passed his bottles to one of the men, grabbed Liv's hand, and tugged her outside before leading her into a densely wooded area. "We need to hurry."

"Roen, this is bad," she said, once again trying to keep up with his long strides. "Do you think you have enough water for everyone?"

He ducked under a branch and held it up long enough for her to pass. "I don't know. But if she hits us with another wave of whateverthehell this is, we're screwed."

"Why don't you just ask the island what she wants?" she panted, jogging behind him after he passed.

She still couldn't believe what she'd witnessed. Between that and the Love Boat massacre this morning, she didn't think she'd ever sleep normally again.

Roen mumbled a long string of swear words. "Can we focus on finding your sister? Because I need to find the elders, and then—" He paused for several moments. "Dammit, woman. Why didn't you agree to sex earlier?" He grumbled something about crisis and trying to think with an erection and how there wasn't time.

"Umm…" *Because now I know something horrible is coming, and I really might not see you again.* "I'm sorry. I know my timing was bad. Forget I said anything."

"Like hell I will," he growled. "You opened the door, and I want in."

Okay. That was an interesting metaphor.

Roen and Liv came upon a grass clearing containing a small, windowless brick shack, about ten by ten feet. He yanked open the steel door, flipped on a light switch, and then grabbed a set of keys hanging on the wall.

"The holding cells are down there." He pointed down a narrow staircase. "Wait here while I look."

Liv watched him disappear and held her breath, listening for any sign of Dana. "Roen?" She popped her index finger into her mouth and nibbled on the nail.

"Liv!" she heard Roen call.

She hurried down the stairs, turned the corner, and entered the cement-floored room with prison cells laid out along the edges, about twelve in total. Shane stood inside a cell with his hands on the bars. Dana stood outside, looking guilty as hell.

"What are you doing here, Dana?" Liv was furious. Why didn't Dana ever listen?

Because she's your sister?

"I needed to see him and hear his voice," Dana replied sheepishly.

"What can I say?" Shane said, his voice low and cocky. "I'm irresistible."

Liv stormed to his cell. "You! You disgusting pig. Stay away from my sister or so help me, Shane, I will go mermaid on your ass."

Shane laughed.

"Liv," Dana protested, "it's not his fault. I came to him, remember?"

"Because he's brainwashed you," she replied. "They have that effect on women."

"Then why aren't I into that one?" Dana pointed to Roen. "Or that one." She pointed to Jason, who sat on the cot in his cell across the room, enjoying the show. "Okay. Never mind. I'm into them, too." She sighed.

"Dana," Liv shook her head, "these are not nice men. That one," Liv pointed to Shane, "tried to drown me. He kidnapped us from our parents' anniversary party."

Dana rolled her eyes. "And he apologized for tha—"

"He was about to make me have sex with him in public to provoke Roen into a fight."

Dana's eyes lit up with fury, and she swiveled toward Shane. "You were going to have sex with my sister?"

Shane shrugged. "Maybe. I am a merman. We don't get a lot of catfish, if yanno what I mean."

"You're disgusting." Liv grabbed Dana's hand. "And this conversation is over. Time to go."

Dana reluctantly started to follow when Roen asked if everyone still had water rations. They replied, "Some but not much."

"Why? What's going on?" Shane asked.

"The pool of sacred water has dried up and the men are being afflicted with some sort of madness."

Shane rubbed his short black beard in a pleased sort of way. "So we have maids who now swim in sunlight, and mermen who are being driven mad. Sounds like the island is sending you a clear message about who's really in control."

"We're not backing down. Whatever the price, things must change," Roen said sternly.

"Hmmm…" Shane said. "If only you knew what might get her to agree to what you're after."

"And you do?" Roen asked distrustfully.

"Yes, and if you let us out, I'll tell you what she wants, since we all know she no longer speaks to you."

"Roen," Liv protested, "he can't be trusted to—"

Roen held out his hand. "He's required to tell me the truth, or I'm permitted to execute him on the spot."

"What does she want?" Roen asked.

"Let me out," Shane replied smugly.

Roen still held the keys in his hand and reached to unlock the cage.

"Don't, Roen!" Liv protested.

Roen pulled her aside and whispered in her ear, "As vile and underhanded as his behavior with you was, he didn't break any of our laws, Liv. The elders say I must let him go. Might as well get something for it."

Liv snarled, "How about I get to kill him? That's something." Sadly, she almost meant it. Shane was dangerous.

"Yes. That certainly would be," Roen agreed, "though it will have to wait."

"I heard that," Shane called out, still grinning like the asshole that he was. "I have to say, my feelings are hurt, Liv. I thought we had something special."

To Roen's credit, he ignored Shane's juvenile taunt and stuck to business, opening the cage. "All right, Shane. What will get her to change her mind?"

Shane strutted out and bellied up to Roen, who was about four inches shorter but twenty times more intimidating, further proof that real strength came from the inside.

"She wants me to take leadership," Shane said.

"I already said you can have it," Roen pointed out. "And I suggest you back off before I break one of your legs."

Shane laughed and stepped back. "Glad you're up for a fight because that's what she wants, for me to challenge you according to our laws. Otherwise, the men will not consider me the rightful leader. If you do that, the island will agree to consider a more peaceful solution along with some of your changes."

"Like what?" asked Roen.

"Like reconsidering spreading this madness."

Roen seemed skeptical. "What about freeing the men and the maids?"

Shane shrugged. "I don't know. But seems to me having the door opened for a discussion is better than drowning in a pissing match."

"Why would she give in so easily?" Roen asked, clearly taking everything Shane said with a brick of salt.

"Who said she's giving in?" Shane replied. "The Big Girl wants something. But hey—feel free to continue on your path. In which case, she says that the humans—" he glanced at Liv " all of them, will start going mad, just like you saw happen to the men today. First, it will hit the coastal areas nearest us and then spread with the rain."

Liv gasped. "Why would she do that?"

Shane shrugged. "Because she can."

"I can't believe this. You're a disgusting bitch!" Liv yelled. "Do you hear me?"

Roen grabbed her arm and squeezed. "Liv, don't provoke her. It won't do any good."

"I'm not going to cower to a bully. Because that's what she is."

Roen actually smiled for a second. She wondered why.

"I like her," Shane said. "She's got balls. Maybe as part of the package, the island will spare her. What do you think, Roen? All you gotta do is fight me."

"Fine. Summon the elders so we may begin the discussion of terms." Roen gestured for Liv and Dana to leave, following closely behind them like a protective watchdog.

"Ten minutes, Roen!" Shane called out. "See you in ten minutes."

Under his breath, Roen cursed something about never getting a break and sex and aching balls and living in a *foking* hell. "Very well. See you in ten."

Dana glanced over her shoulder at Shane and then asked Liv, "Why do I still want him? He's so awful."

"I don't know," Liv said, while they made their way out of the prison.

Once outside, Roen headed in the direction of his house. The late afternoon sun had replaced the drizzling gray clouds.

"Wait," Liv called to Roen, whose panicked expression had turned to full-blown warpath. "Are you serious about fighting Shane?"

"Yes." He stopped briefly so she and Dana could catch up. "First, I'm going to get you both back safely to my home."

"What if he wins?" Liv asked.

Roen's normally supple lips flattened into a thin, hard line.

Liv held up her hands. "Sorry. Of course you can kick his ass." While both men fell into the "fierce warrior" category, Roen had a vibe that…well, he just had a vibe. Indestructible, larger than life, fearless. Shane was more of the shady type one expected to see in a dark alley, jumping out of the shadows, which made Shane more dangerous in some ways because he didn't play by the same rules.

That wave of dread hit Liv once more, telling her a devastating event was charging in their direction, like some hideous runaway freight train filled with doom.

"I'm coming with you," she argued.

He sighed with agitation. "I have to go and settle this. And you would only be a…" His eyes wandered down to the stretchy black fabric hugging her breasts.

Liv dipped her head to intercept his gaze. "I'm guessing you were about to say 'distraction.'"

Roen vigorously shook his head from side to side. "Yes. Exactly. Dana will also be safer in my house, and she cannot be left alone right now."

"Okay," Liv conceded reluctantly. "But promise you won't do any fighting tonight." That dark cloud kept nudging the back of her mind.

Oh God. Please let me be wrong. I just want more time with him. Please. Additionally, if she could figure out Crazy Dirt's vulnerabilities, it might change the entire game. Roen wouldn't have to fight anyone.

Roen replied, "It will likely happen tomorrow. Time is of the essence."

Liv's heart instantly felt like a bag of wet sand. If Roen lost, Shane wasn't about to show him mercy. He would be dead. Dead. She couldn't bear the thought and neither could her heart. No, she could survive almost anything, but not that. Then there was the little issue pertaining to Dana because, frankly, Liv didn't think she'd care so much about herself in that scenario; she'd be too heartbroken. But Dana?

This goddamned nightmare just won't end. To the contrary, it kept getting uglier.

When Roen deposited them at his front door, he grabbed Liv by the waist and pulled her tightly against his hard frame. He kissed her, and her entire body melted into him. The taste of this man was like chocolate and red wine and those little lavender flowers that only bloomed in her mother's garden in late spring and the smell of crisp fresh air and the sound of her family laughing around the dinner table, topped with a case study of an ancient civilization—all of her favorite things in this world rolled into one.

This is meant to be. It can't end. It can't... Liv sucked up the urge to cry.

He slowly pulled away and bent his head toward her ear. "Don't think I've forgotten what you've promised me, Liv. I'm going to settle the details of the challenge, and then I'm coming straight back here to foke you like an animal—per your request."

Liv gulped. "Don't for-for-get-get the making love and—oh, never mind. It's a date." She pushed the air back into her lungs.

Roen strutted away and Liv watched in utter fascination. While she appreciated those tanned broad shoulders and muscles rippling under the tight skin of his back, it was his determination and strength, his hard outer shell he used to shield and protect anyone and everything he cared about, that made her swoon. He was such a contrast to the man once deemed "soulless and money grubbing" by the media. Somehow, he'd found himself in this hellhole and become the most beautiful, sexy man she'd ever known.

I have to do something to save him. I have to.

"How come you got to fall in love with the nice one, and I got to fall in love with the bad one?" Dana asked, who'd been standing there the entire time.

Liv winced. "You are not in love, you idiot. You're in…" What was the right word? "Mer-lust."

CHAPTER FIFTEEN

After an hour-long heated debate in the great hall, where the healed men still buzzed after the "attack," Roen, Shane, and the elders reached an agreement with the island via Naylor, who spoke for Her Majesty.

No, Roen didn't feel at all satisfied with the outcome; however, the compromise would spare lives.

Except mine.

Roen should've known Shane would find some obscure law to circumvent a direct physical fight. Shane, after all, was a coward. And this was the one challenge Roen could not think or fight his way out of. *Foking Shane.*

The only silver lining out of all this was that in exchange for "fighting" Shane, the island would halt her attack. Upon Shane's victory, she would also agree to honor the original deal struck by their ancestors and allow any man who had sons on the island to leave with their mates. In other words, a merman could leave if he produced a replacement—that had been the deal. How many mermen qualified? They'd have to do a little work to figure that out. In most cases, they had no clue who'd fathered who. Their mothers swore—at risk of death—never to speak of the island or the men. That included mentioning Dear Old Dad. "What assurances do we have that our men won't die before having the opportunity to leave?" Roen had asked. They lost men all the time in challenges or executions due to their extremely rigid, antiquated laws. The island's response sounded too good to be true: killing, including fighting to the death, would be banned.

Did Roen trust the island wouldn't double-cross him? No. However, he had two choices: continue on his path or this. Hell, if she backed out, their people always had the option to return to outright defiance. The potential gain was worth the risk.

All that said, Roen couldn't deny he remained on the fence, still wanting in his heart to finish what he started; however, the island made one final offer he couldn't pass up. It was the one thing he wanted more than anything…

Roen entered his home, detesting what would come next.

He found Liv and Dana in the library, heatedly debating the island's powers. Both had their hair pulled into ponytails and wore those snug black dresses, but something about seeing that outfit on Liv's feminine figure nearly undid him every time. *God, those curves.*

His memories of every woman he'd ever been with during his shallow, human days had been completely erased from his mind, replaced by images of the most stunning woman in the world. Liv. He would regret never showing her how much he truly loved her. *You'll be showing her in a moment. And someday, she will come to understand that.*

"Hello, Liv," Roen said in his most confident, non-alarming voice.

"Roen! What happened?" Liv jumped from the couch and ran to him.

He glanced over at Dana. "If you don't mind, I'd like to speak with Liv for a moment."

"Oh. I can leave," offered Dana.

Roen held up his hand. "And have you run off again, looking for Shane? No."

Dana smiled guiltily. "I'll take anyone. You, for example, are really, really ho—"

"Let's go." Liv took Roen's hand and pulled him outside, shutting the library doors behind them. He found it adorable when she behaved possessively.

"So?" She crossed her arms over her chest. Perhaps to keep him focused. He truly loved staring at her beautiful round…

"Roen?" Liv huffed impatiently, pulling him away from his lusty thoughts.

"Ah. Yes. I have news."

"Spit it out." Her brown eyes sparkled with so much life, so much hope and determination.

She truly is a work of art.

"It's complicated," he said.

"Oh no." She covered her mouth. "It's going to be some squirrelly island deal, isn't it?"

"Squirrelly is not the word I would choose. Complicated with many pros versus cons might be more appropriate."

Liv placed her hand over her heart. "Oh God. I'm so relieved. I thought you were going to give me bad news."

He was. He absolutely was. And his heart felt like it might crack right down the middle because of it.

He continued. "There are several parts to the agreement; however, she has agreed to halt the attack on the men and landlovers. Also, the water will flow again."

"That's great! She knows she can't kill you all off."

Rocn gave her a hushing glare.

"Sorry. I'll let you finish." Liv twisted an invisible key over her tantalizing puckered lips and threw it onto the ground, followed by a stomp, stomp.

Roen continued, "She has also agreed to honor an old agreement with our elders that allows for some of the men to leave with their mates. In exchange for these things, she wishes me to accept Shane's challenge so he'll have the opportunity to lead without the men questioning his strength. Of course, you know I've already consented to this, and if the island no longer wishes the Dorans to lead, then who am I to argue?"

"Are you done? 'Cause I have a question."

He already knew what she wanted to ask. "The answer is no. I will not be permitted to live if Shane is victorious."

Liv's eyes filled with tears.

He added, "She feels extremely threatened by her inability to control me."

"Wh-what if you win?" Liv asked.

Roen looked away. "I cannot win. This is the unspoken part of the agreement. My people's freedom will only be honored after Shane is in power."

The news instantly shredded Liv's heart to ribbons. "This is what I was afraid of." This was the something bad that would separate them. Permanently.

Oh God. What am I going to do? I can't lose him. I can't.

"An-and Dana?" Liv stuttered.

Roen looked down at the tiled floor, rubbing the tip of his thick strong fingers over the rich brown whiskers on his chin. "You and Dana are to be exiled from the island. No one may ever bring you back."

Coming to grips with the full meaning of what Roen had said, tears filled Liv's eyes. Lives would be saved, some of his men and their mates would be set free, and Liv and Dana would go home. *Roen's life is the price.*

"You can't accept, Roen. Tell her no."

"It's far better than watching my men suffer and slit their own throats. It's best for your people, too."

Yes, but she suspected—she knew—his instincts to keep her safe had been a factor. Had she not been part of the equation, Roen might have chosen to stick to his guns and free everyone once and for all.

"You know you can't trust her, Roen. The minute you're gone, she'll change her mind."

He nodded solemnly, his green eyes washing over with a haze of deep pain. "Either way, I'll be gone, which means you'll be safe. You will serve no purpose to her, and my death will sever the bond between us."

No. Dammit. No. She couldn't accept this. And she couldn't allow him to accept this bullshit deal because of her. Her being there had made him weak, exactly like he'd said.

She wasn't to blame, though. No. Fact: Liv hadn't come to the island of her own free will. Fact: the island had manipulated Shane, the greedy bastard, to steal Liv away and bring her back, likely promising to make his dream of leading come true. Fact: the island then pushed and pulled and maneuvered the outcome, every step of the way, ensuring that Liv would serve her desired purpose: to control Roen. Dana had been brought along as leverage against herself. And what did the island really want? She guessed for Roen to stop trying to change things.

Fail. It didn't work. Roen couldn't be so easily swayed, which likely shifted her plans to destroying him. *That's what I'd do if I were a power-hungry demon from hell.*

Yes, the island played a mean and evil game of Battleship, and it was a consistent one. *She uses love as her weapon.* Not physical strength (because she had none) or intelligence (that was a giant question mark). Only love. The men's love of their maids. Roen's love of his people. Roen's error had been trying to play according to a noble set of rules. Only, it seemed the island's view into their hearts was more of a one-way deal. They couldn't see into hers, giving the evil bitch the advantage. *And she takes and she takes and she takes…*

That's when the lightning bolt struck. Roen mentioned their scientists weren't able to figure out how the island sustained herself, and the old bitch wasn't giving them any help. So what if, just what if…the island's source of power didn't come from some unknown mystical place, but from these men? Hadn't that old legend she'd read—about that Segar Doran guy—say these people once had the power to move oceans and control the sky and that those powers disappeared?

Then Roen's men revolted and the water stopped flowing. *She masks it by trying to make it look like a punishment.*

Yes. This had to be it. *They try to leave; Crazy Dirt reels them right back, using every weapon in her arsenal—threats.* When threats didn't work, she switched gears to promises of happy times and freedom. She'd do or say anything to prevent them from leaving.

Could it be possible? The island is some leechlike creature and nothing more? No other explanation fit.

The only question Liv had now was whether life on Earth really depended on her "spark," or was that another lie meant to validate the elaborate web of deceit she'd created? *Give them a purpose, something to fight for and believe in.*

It was like a goddamned religious cult, every one of the men so brainwashed and blinded by duty, tradition, and folklore they never questioned why any of them were really there. *And what greater purpose is there than believing your race is the guardian of all life on the planet?*

Which meant they had way more power than they realized, because they were her fuel. *I bet it's the reason she helps them get so big. Drink your water, boys, so you grow up big and strong so I can suck the life from you.* Roen was probably some giant, irresistible morsel of power she'd wanted in her stable, and then quickly figured out he was too strong. *Untamable.*

And finally, it seemed odd to Liv that there were so few mermen, especially compared to the number of mermaids. If protection was Crazy Dirt's main concern, then why allow these men to kill each other off? Wouldn't more be better?

It's easier to control smaller numbers. Liv didn't know for sure, but her head tingled like a bag of wet Pop Rocks. *I'm definitely onto something.*

Liv looked at Roen and was about to tell him that her big beautiful landlover brain had figured out the island's game, when Roen grabbed her and kissed her. His strong arms held her so tight she felt his heart plucking away inside his chest. His lips, however, moved unhurriedly over her mouth, gently sliding and pushing, allowing her to savor the silky heat of his lips. Meanwhile, his short rich-brown beard tickled the edges of her mouth, creating a kiss of tender roughness. This kiss was everything Roen. Domineering and sensual, sweet and prickly. This was a kiss she'd remember until her last dying breath, but one wasn't enough. She wanted a lifetime of these kisses.

Roen abruptly broke away and stared deeply into her eyes. Love. There was so much love staring back at her. Then he looked over her shoulder and nodded. Before she saw who stood there, a large hand covered her mouth, and a strong arm gripped her waist.

"Take her to the plane," Roen ordered. "And have Edward handcuff her to the seat. Then come back for her sister. You do not stop for anything or anyone. Do you hear me? Make sure the pilot knows to take her straight to my office in Seattle—my lawyer will take care of the rest."

Liv twisted and tried to yell, "Wha-ow-you doey?" *What are you doing?*

Roen gazed into her eyes. "I'm sorry, Liv. Shane challenged me to the Great Swim. I only have a few hours to prepare everything to ensure you will be all right after I'm gone."

What the fuck?

"No. No! I harf to ter you somming." *I have to tell you something.* "Yo herf ooood!" *You're her food.*

"I know you're upset, but I have no choice. I love you, Liv. More than you could ever possibly understand. My only regret was not getting to treat you like an animal." He flashed a devilish smile and turned away. Somehow she knew it was only for show, perhaps meant to comfort her in some small way—to show her he'd be okay.

Dammit, she had to tell him what she'd figured out. He shouldn't back down. No. He should do the opposite. If Liv was right, then they held the cards. They only needed to wait it out until that bitch lost her steam.

"Roeyy! No!" she mumbled, but he was long gone.

The man behind her dragged her out the front door and threw her over his shoulder, placing her high above the ground. "Godfuckingdammit. What is wrong with you people?"

"Shut the foke up."

Liv recognized that deep, deep voice. "Lyle?"

"L'isle," he corrected. "And my brother is about to die, so I really don't want to hear any of your landlover bullcrap."

"Lyle, you have…to…listen…to me." Her body bounced on his big shoulder, making it difficult to breathe.

"No."

"I've figured out…the island. She needs…you. She feeds…off you like a giant…parasite."

Lyle stopped, and she squirmed and pushed with her hands.

"Please. You need to tell Roen to hold his ground. She isn't making water because you've all turned on her. Think about it. She's like a child who feeds off attention and doesn't want to share it with anyone. That's why she makes your women suffer. That's why she will never let anyone go free."

Lyle slid her off his shoulder. "How do you know this?"

"I've been studying relationships and how they influence cultural development for years."

"And you think the island feeds off of us?" he said quietly, his eyes shifting from side to side.

"It explains where her power comes from and why she does all of these crazy things to keep you near her. You're like her food."

Lyle blinked his green eyes at her and that's when she noticed they were the same as Roen's. "We need to find Roen quic—"

Something long and hard hit Lyle over the head.

Liv screamed and turned, terrified to find the bane of her existence standing there with a shit-eating grin. "What did you do?" She kneeled down to look at Lyle's head. Blood flowed from a deep gash onto the stones of the walkway. "Do you have any water? He might die." She glanced up at Shane's triumphant smile.

"Then he dies. A small price to pay to get what I want."

"Killing another merman in cold blood is against your laws. And didn't Roen make a deal to let me go?"

Shane wagged his finger. "Sorry. There's been a change of plans."

"I knew Roen shouldn't have let you out. And for the record, what I said to you the day we met still stands. I'd rather slit my own throat."

He shook his head at the ground. "Oh, Liv. Tsk, tsk, tsk. You think I really want someone like you? *I'm* too fucking good for you. You're a criminal."

"What are you talking about?" She stepped back only to realize half of the Shane Gang stood behind her.

"Oh, you'll see," Shane said. "We reserve the best punishments for landlovers like you who break our highest law."

She had no clue what he meant, and somehow it didn't matter. He wasn't there to reason with her.

"What about Dana?" she asked.

"Not sure yet. You, on the other hand…your fate has been sealed."

CHAPTER SIXTEEN

While Roen waited in the great hall for Shane, his heart filled with relief and joy with the sound of the airplane's engine roaring overhead. Liv and Dana were on their way home. And with him dead, Liv would be free—the island would no longer have a purpose for her, and she would not go crazy from their separation. Once one's mate died, the bond died, too. Yes, Liv was saved—something to be proud of—and she would be well taken care of because he'd left everything to her. "Are you out of your fucking mind, Ro?" his lawyer Phil had said. "You're going to leave your fortune to that little piece of ass? Wow. She must've been really great in bed."

Roen didn't reply, other than to say, "Phil, you're a pig, but you've been a good friend. Almost like a brother. Except you're an even bigger asshole."

"Wait. So…so…this is goodbye? Are you dying? Is it cancer?" Phil had asked, sounding genuinely concerned. A first.

"No," he lied, "I'm fine. Just promise if anything happens to me and Liv ever needs help, you'll do what you can."

"Uh—uh…" Phil had blown out a long, hollow breath. "Yeah, sure, Ro. Whatever she needs."

"Thank you, Phil. Now get the hell back to work." Roen had hung up the phone and grinned, remembering every fire they'd put out and every other hurdle they'd fought over the years. He would miss that bastard.

In the case of Lyle—his brother, his family, his blood—Roen had tried to reason with him and get him to leave with Liv and Dana, but Lyle made it clear that his only regret in life had been living so many years without his brother at his side. "I will wait for your return," Lyle had said.

"Lyle, you and I both know I'm not coming back," Roen had responded. "And once I'm gone, Shane will find an excuse to kill you."

"Then so be it, brother. I will be here waiting all the same."

Roen embraced his brother quickly, regretting that they'd not once spoken about the past, including what happened to Lyle during the time Roen believed him to be dead or how Lyle came to be on the island in the first place. There was so much left unspoken between the two, but neither had been eager to dredge up the past. They'd both found peace in being reunited. Still, Roen now wished they'd had that talk.

After their embrace, Lyle went with him to retrieve Liv. His brother would see her and Dana safely onto the plane while Roen went to meet his fate. There would be no time for goodbyes.

Add that regret to the pile, Roen thought to himself when Shane strutted into the great hall, a smug smile stretched across his face. Naylor and ten of Shane's men followed closely behind, in show of their support.

I wonder what Shane promised them. None of that mattered now; the cards were dealt.

Roen cleared his throat to address his men one last time. "Mermen, I want you to know how much I truly honor the faith you've put in me. And today is no different. If I don't return, it means that Shane is the stronger merman and more fit to lead you according to the time-honored traditions of the island."

Unexpectedly, the one hundred and ninety fierce men—covered in tattoos and scars, some holding weapons—began chanting Roen's name while scowling at Shane. They saw right through the lie. What could Roen do now? Let the island kill Liv or continue to punish them all?

Shane laughed. "Well, we all know how this will end. So I'm confident in saying that when I return, I'll restore order among us. Because I have confirmation that the island's fears of a landlover invasion are indeed accurate. Now is the time for us to unite. Everyone should be preparing, and when I return, we will finalize our plan of attack."

"What do you mean?" Roen asked. "What confirmation?"

"Ah. You see? The fact that you don't know is proof you are unfit to lead. Not to worry, I'll make sure the landlovers are dealt with and that the island doesn't wipe out humanity. Because unlike you, she trusts me to take care of her."

Roen wanted to strangle the man. Shane wasn't fit to lead a box of Twinkies. *He doesn't care about anyone but himself.*

Of course, only a few short months ago, when he'd come to the shores of this strange place, Roen hadn't cared about anyone else either. He'd been a broken man, his soul coated in hate and disdain for the world. Liv, he realized, changed all that. She'd reconnected him to his heart and, through her, the rest of the world. That first day they'd met, she'd reached inside him and illuminated his soul with the simple act of opening her beautiful brown eyes and gazing right through the scar tissue. "You're the most misjudged man I've ever met," she'd said.

Roen's heart warmed with the memory, and standing there among these loyal men, the truth came down on him like an ocean freighter. Becoming leader of this place had been his calling, but Liv had been his destiny. *And now you will die a whole man with a whole heart.* He only wished he'd had the chance to thank her for that.

"Shane," Roen dipped his head, "I sincerely wish you luck. May you find everything you're looking for." Roen then turned to the men and gave them a final nod. The look of fury in their eyes pained him, but this wasn't something he could change now.

Roen stripped off his suede and Shane removed the cloth around his waist. The two turned to Naylor, who stood in front of Roen's throne, looking like a desiccated version of the men in the room—thin and bony, white hair and beard, saggy skin.

Naylor hacked out a phlegm ball from his throat, and the room fell from angry mumbles to complete silence. "A challenge for leadership of the island has been issued by Shane. Per the laws written in our ancient scriptures, a merman may challenge for leadership through use of fists, sword, or dagger. However, considering we are sons of the sea, the time-honored tradition of physical stamina may also be used to prove one's worthiness above another." Naylor's cold, ancient gaze of deep green swept the room. "Two thousand miles of ocean. The first man to return alive will be our leader. The second man will be sacrificed to the maids if he has not already perished during the journey. If neither man returns, leadership will open to anyone strong enough and willing to claim it."

Roen's stomach twisted into a knot. Surely the island had provided Shane the idea to challenge him this way. It was so ancient that even Naylor had had to look it up before declaring it valid.

It was quite the genius move, really, considering the island's motive to produce a genuine victory.

Fist fighting, for example, wouldn't have been a sure thing.

But this... Roen loathed swimming and detested the ocean even more. Yes, he realized how odd that seemed. Nevertheless, he and Lyle weren't allowed anywhere near it because of their mother's fear of the ocean. Later in life, Roen took private swimming lessons in a pool only because he never wanted to be in a situation where he looked like an idiot. What sort of grown man couldn't swim and had a pool in almost every home he owned? Since coming to the island, he'd been practicing a bit here and there—including diving; however, a mediocre swimmer would never make it two thousand miles.

Naylor went on, "Each man must reach Nitrof Point on the island of Amatignak, retrieve a white pebble from its shore, and journey home."

Amatignak was part of the Derlof Islands in Alaska. Except for the occasional biologists or tourists, the island was completely uninhabited. Not that it mattered, because he knew he'd never make it that far. If by some miracle he did, Shane would be far ahead.

Maybe I'll get lucky and a whale will eat him, Roen thought, then pulled himself back. The deal had been struck with the island, and though no words were spoken, Roen understood he could not win. That was the reason the island agreed to his terms.

"May the spirits of our ancestors be with you, mermen," Naylor declared.

Roen took a deep breath and headed for the shore. Once there, he gazed up at the early evening sky glimmering with flaming orange, and said goodbye to Liv one last time, wishing her a beautiful life full of hope and love and everything she dreamed of.

I will miss you, landlover, with all my heart.

A few hours after being dragged away from Lyle, an older man with long, fluffy white hair and a beard to match entered the prison, where she'd been screaming at the top of her lungs for someone—anyone to let her out. Yes, it was the same prison she'd been in earlier that day with the cement floors and twelve cells.

"Hello, Liv. My name is Naylor, I am an elder here on this island, and in the absence of our leader, I am charged with administering the laws."

Liv got up from the army green cot she'd been sitting on. "Where's Roen?" she asked, grabbing the bars of her cell.

"Gone," answered Naylor, "to face his fate."

"Is he…is he…" She couldn't say it.

"Dead?" the man said for her. "Not yet, but he soon will be."

She gripped the bars firmly to hold herself upright. She didn't know how to describe what was happening inside her, but it felt like her heart was suffocating and collapsing in on itself under the weight of her rage. Pure, ugly, hateful rage.

"And Dana?"

"Dana's life has been spared, and she's left the island."

That was surely a good thing, but it didn't take away the fact that Roen was about to die.

He went on, "In your case, dear, I'm afraid the deal Roen struck cannot be honored. It has come to our attention that you have broken our most sacred law. For this, you shall be executed."

Liv's eyes narrowed. "What did I do?"

"You think because we are here, isolated from your world, that we do not monitor what happens? We make it our business to know everything—do not let our primitive dress fool you, Liv." Naylor made a juicy cough and then swallowed the glob.

"You can save the superiority lectures," Liv said acrimoniously, "and tell me what the fuck you think I've done so we can get this over with."

"In such a hurry to die?" Naylor said.

"No. I'm sick and tired of these games, especially the island's. I mean, really. She has you idiots so wrapped up in myths and archaic traditions that you've all become blind to the fact that she has absolutely zero control over you."

Naylor gave her a look like he wanted to carry out the execution right then and there.

"Oh no—" Liv threw up her hands "—did the silly landlover upset you? Or is the island buzzing away in your ears right now, telling you I'm a liar?"

"Are you claiming you're not?" he asked with a condescending smile.

"Yes. I'm also free of any brainwashing because I haven't been digesting a steady diet of bullshit for hundreds of generations. You do not need her to survive. She needs you. She feeds off of you."

"You were right, my dear," Naylor said, shaking his bony finger, "you are a silly landlover. Because without her, life on Earth cannot survive. She is the key to the circle of life."

Liv wasn't so sure about that.

"Looks more to me like a food chain than a circle. And you are higher up, yet you insist on letting her pretend it's the other way around. But I *will* hand it to her; she's a master manipulator. She made all these rules and you guys follow her like sheep. Meanwhile, the only rule she obeys is keeping herself on top."

Naylor cocked his head. "Your attempt to circumvent death is understandable. But I will not allow you to dishonor us with your insults."

Liv lifted her chin, gripping the bars. "They're the truth."

"The only part of your logic I agree with is that there is a pecking order among life on this planet. And your species is somewhere beneath the cockroach."

Liv laughed and crossed her arms. "Oh really? Then how come you need us to have children and to guard your island? You can't have babies on your own. And your history proves that you men can't protect the island on your own. I believe the name 'El Corazón' was meant to remind you of that." Yeah, the men had their butts kicked by Spanish explorers, and the maids saved the day. "So without us landlover-ladies, you'd all die off. Therefore, in the scheme of things, I'd argue you're beneath me. You, your men, and your fucking idiot of an island. The only person who was worth a damn was Roen, but you just proved your superiority by fucking that one up, too. What a bunch of asshats." Liv released an accomplished sigh and grinned. "Okay. Now I'm ready to die."

Naylor's nostrils flared with abhorrence and his pale wrinkly skin flushed. "Seems we agree on something." He called out over his shoulder and two men appeared, one being Jason.

"Throw her to the maids," Naylor ordered.

"Wait!" Liv said. "You never told me what I did."

"You gave a landlover—a doctor Fuller—a sample of our water. She's made public claims that she's discovered a substance that can cure any illness."

Dr. Fuller had attended to her and Dana after they'd both had "episodes." First Liv then Dana. After running blood tests and discovering an unknown substance in Liv's system, Dana then experienced a very suspicious attack and ended up in the ER later that night. Liv miraculously had sacred water on hand to save Dana.

What a conniving bitch! No, Liv didn't know how the island had gotten to Dana and made her sick to begin with, but it all felt like another well-orchestrated event. The strangest part was that three weeks later, Dr. Fuller confronted Liv with more lab tests and told her she'd dreamed of the "miracle drug" found in her blood. Liv chalked it up to a nosy doctor and coincidence. Now Liv knew that was ridiculous.

"Well," Liv sighed, "I realize no one is interested in the real story, so I'll just say that I didn't tell or give anything to Dr. Fuller. Regardless, the circumstances miraculously played out in favor of D.B."

"Who is D.B.?"

"Your island. I've renamed her Dirty Bitch. Because she's made of dirt. And she's a bitch. I'm hoping it will stick like the El Corazón name."

Naylor left, shaking his head, while Jason and the other man stayed behind.

"What are you waiting for, Jason?" Liv snarled. "Throw me to the maids."

A moment of regret flickered in his green eyes. "I'm sorry, Liv."

"Is that sorry enough to let me go?" she asked.

"No. I cannot disobey orders." He glanced down at his bare feet.

"Then let's get this over with."

When they took her from the holding cell, she felt tempted to make sheep sounds to taunt them, but she wanted to use her few remaining moments to think of the truly wonderful things in her life: those whom she loved, especially Roen. She remembered coming across a story in one of the texts in the library about how the mermen believed they would be united in the afterlife with their mates. The sketches in the book were of a man and a woman, nude and embracing on a beach, passionately kissing in a *From Here to Eternity* moment. She remembered sighing, thinking how wonderful it would be if something that sinful awaited everyone after they passed on. *An eternal make-out session with the man you loved.*

She straightened her spine. *Think of that, Liv. Think of being with Roen, in his arms, kissing his lips. Just think of that.*

The two men walked with Liv to the beach, where the final rays of sunlight sank into the horizon. They called out in a strange language reminding her of Greek or Latin. Within seconds, yellow eyes and reams of flowing black hair rose like a haunting nightmare from the calm waves.

Liv's urge to run for her life kicked in right when the men threw her in. Claws dug into her flesh and razor-sharp teeth bit into her arms and legs. She screamed, but the salty water entered her mouth and smothered her voice.

CHAPTER SEVENTEEN

Roen had been swimming less than ten hours when his body finally gave out. Exhausted, he flipped onto his back and stared up at the early morning sky. The pastel blue seemed so flat and mundane compared to the sky over the island, and he welcomed the hell out of it.

"Aah!" A cramp shot through his leg. Every muscle felt like he'd put them through a meat grinder. His skin felt raw from the exposure to the salt. His lungs burned from a night of inhaling, and then coughing out, buckets of water.

Meanwhile, Shane was well on his way to Amatignak. *Hell, he's probably there by now.* For the record, the fastest humans swam an average of four point five miles per hour—not much faster than speed-walking. It would take that same person eighteen days to make a two-thousand-mile journey if they somehow swam nonstop. Impossible, of course. A well-trained merman like Shane, however, swam ten miles per hour, which meant he'd make the two-thousand-mile journey in a little over eight days.

Whichever way Roen sliced it, there would be no beating Shane even if he wanted to. Which he did not. Roen had come to genuine terms with his fate, settling any remaining thoughts of resistance somewhere between mile three—after he'd miraculously avoided becoming mermaid food—and mile forty when his nature to push back and fight began urging him to turn this around.

Roen, this is the one time you must defy yourself. You cannot back out, because you know what will happen. Liv would die. The men would suffer.

"You must face the end like a merman with honor and bravery," he mumbled to himself.

"Brave? You are not brave," said a toxic feminine voice. *"You are a worthless, useless traitor, Roen. And now that you see there is no limit to my power, no distance too far, no task too low or cruel to punish those who defy me, I hope your final thoughts will be of me and how you should've bowed down to me, merman."*

Roen held his breath and treaded water, wondering if his mind wasn't playing tricks on him.

"Well? Don't you have anything to say, merman? Perhaps you might start with admitting how wrong you were to break your vow."

"I vowed to protect you and lead those men. I didn't break anything."

"You vowed to give your heart to me! You vowed obedience in exchange for saving that little bitch's

life!" she roared so loudly, his eye sockets reverberated.

"I couldn't. Liv is the only thing in this world I can't live without."

"Because you're weak, Roen. Weak and unfit to lead. Unfit to save anyone. Unfit to live. The same goes for everyone who followed you."

A burning sensation exploded on his face and inside his eyes. He screamed in agony, feeling the sunlight sear straight through his skin and lids, singeing the nerves and muscles. The pain felt like hot oil thrown in the eyes.

"That's right, Roen," she chuckled her words. "*Who's the mighty warrior now? Where are all your ships and your men? How about that money you love so much? I am the only real power."*

Roen instinctively dove down to escape the burning rays of the sun, but the pain wouldn't stop. It was enough to drive a man over the edge and slice his own throat.

Sadly, there were no knives here.

As best as he could, Roen relaxed his body and thought of the beautiful place he'd read about in one of his people's many stories. It was a place where those you loved greeted you with open arms. Where sadness, anger, and regret didn't exist. Suffering was for those in the physical world. Roen was not a religious man, nor could he claim to be spiritual, but imagining such a place gave him comfort. He pictured Liv in a skimpy bikini, running in the waves, her long dark hair blowing in the wind, her smile so bright it could warm the coldest heart. He pictured holding her in his arms and telling her he loved her more than any man had ever loved a woman since the dawn of time. Roen visualized every detail of his perfect world with the woman he loved; meanwhile his body sank lower and lower into the dark, cold, foreboding abyss of the North Pacific.

Just let go, Roen. Let go…

A cool hand on his wrist and the jolting pain of his skin being pierced snapped him into a shallow moment of lucidity. Bright yellow eyes flickered at him.

Was he dreaming?

The mermaid's eyes narrowed, and she dug her nails deep into his arm, eliciting a garbled scream; meanwhile she swam so fast the resistance of the water tugged at his raw, cold skin.

His head broke through the surface, and the maid slammed her fist straight into his stomach. He coughed hard, projecting a stream of salty water.

The maid released her grip and cupped his face, staring deeply into his eyes. "We count on you. Save us," she said in a scratchy, nearly inaudible animal voice. "You fight, merman. And you fucking swim."

What the foke?

"You know I was trying to help you?" he asked.

The maid nodded. "Swim."

How could he?

"Who are you?" he asked. More importantly, why hadn't she eaten him?

"Swim, merman! You win," she replied, pulling him along.

He spit some water from his mouth. "I can't win," he panted, waves splashing his face. "And if I could, the island will know you helped me. Either way, I lose." *Then she'll go back to punishing everyone*. If she wasn't planning to do that already.

"She can't hurt them," said the maid with her unnatural voice, "if they don't let her."

"What did you say?"

The maid stopped swimming and carefully pushed out her words. "Shut her out. Shut her out."

"What do you mean?"

The maid poked at the skin over his heart. "Close here. You let in. You push out."

The mermaid's words kicked down the walls of the dark cave he'd been living in since coming to the island. He had chosen to let the island in the night he fought for leadership. He had decided. *He* let her into his heart. So it only served to reason he could shut her out, and if he could, they all could.

"Wait," he told the maid. Roen clenched his eyes shut and attempted to imagine his heart closing, but nothing happened.

He opened his eyes. "I'm not sure I know how," he said to the maid.

The maid swam a few laps around his body and then popped her head up. "Speak to her. Say she must go." The maid pointed to his head and poked him with her black claw.

He thought he understood what she meant—tell her to leave. Plain and simple. But could it be that? So simple? It was worth a try.

This time Roen closed his eyes and silently said, *I no longer accept you. You are no longer welcome in my heart. I revoke my connection with you.* He visualized the doors in his heart slamming shut and blocking out the intruder.

Light instantly poured inside his mind, filling every dark corner with vivid clarity. Every minute of every day for the last three months had been shrouded in a murky cloud. "Bloody hell. She's been blinding me." Fresh images and thoughts flashed inside Roen's head. He now understood everything he'd seen and learned—the texts, scrolls, folklore, and stories. The conversations he'd had with his men and the elders. He'd been working for months learning everything he could, but somehow the island had kept him from connecting any dots. *Like little foking partitions in my head.*

The answers were right in front of him the entire time.

"We're all afraid of her. An island." He laughed. Yet, she had no hands to punch with, no legs to kick with. Her only real means of physical contact was through that water, which they gladly drank every goddamned day—why wouldn't they? It made them strong and indestructible. It made them fearless. He didn't need the island for that. Neither did those men.

Without their willingness to let her in and drink that water, her illusion of control vanished. She could do little more than inflict pain. And death? No. She needed them to do that. Otherwise, she would've mowed men down on her own. It was all one big illusion, masterfully woven with fear and manipulation.

Roen smiled at the bobbing black face snapping her lids open and shut in an awkward birdlike rhythm. "You're a genius," he said. "I think you've figured out how to save us."

She shook her head and growled.

Oh. He hadn't figured out how to save the maids, had he? Thankfully, his mind felt like a razor-sharp sword, ready to cut down anything in his way.

The stories said the women engaged in sex and were bitten. But knowing the island's adeptness at playing smoke and mirrors, what was missing? He'd bitten Liv, and she had been fine. No, they hadn't had sex, but was that really the trigger?

It's the water. Everything led back to the water, and Liv had drunk some before being bitten. In fact, because of her resistance to the water, Holden, their healer, had mentioned in passing how he'd given Liv an entire IV bag full of it before he'd seen an effect on Liv's dehydration that day she'd first come to El Corazón.

Was that the key?

The men's bites had some sort of, well, for lack of a better word, infectious substance, similar to the folklore related to the effects of a vampire or werewolf bite. Of course, those species weren't real. But mermen were. And if the women ingested any of the sacred water, it would prevent their venom or whatever they carried from taking hold.

Now, how it all worked out so that the men's mates didn't drink any sacred water during claiming, he didn't know. There were a million ways the island could rig the "game." For example, he could easily see the old bitch whispering in the men's ears to give their particular woman a sip of water, making the night last much longer. Those women went home thoroughly worked over, filled repeatedly with potent sperm, and ended up pregnant. No surprise there.

Foke. That must be it.

Roen looked at his companion. Her big bright eyes were glued to his face.

"Have you ever been given any sacred water?" he asked.

She held up her sharp claw, trying to form a word. "Swim in sunlight with it."

Roen winced. His arms cramped in the cold water. "You mean, the other day when the ship was attacked, some of the maids drank sacred water?"

The maid nodded. "Caves," she ground out the word. "Filled with it. We drink."

Sonofabitch. The water had disappeared from the pool in the great hall because the island had diverted it into the ocean. The maids, who lived beneath the island, taking shelter in the underwater caves, were flushed with it, which is why they were able to come out into the sunlight and attack the women.

Had the island done it on purpose, knowing that would be the outcome? Perhaps. Regardless, it stood to reason that the women had been partially "cured."

Roen now felt the warmth of full sunlight on the back of his head while his arms made excruciating rotations in the cold, salty water. He looked to his side, and there she was right below the surface, her long, sleek black body floating in the water, her tail undulating like a dolphin's. The sunlight did not seem to affect her one bit.

Roen wanted to scream with joy. He could end this nightmare—permanently—for everyone, including himself. *I can be with Liv,* he realized. *Holy foking hell. I can be with Liv!* This goddamned challenge had turned out to be the biggest damned blessing in disguise of his life.

Roen looked up at the bright blue sky and enjoyed the feel of the sun on his cold, raw face. He felt a hard bump from behind and saw the mermaid snarling, flashing her razor-sharp teeth.

"No." He shook his head at her. "We're turning around."

The maid blinked her big eyes in question. Despite her shocking, monster-like appearance, with the inky jet-black skin and ropes of hair resembling charred seaweed, she was beautiful in an exotic sort of way—high cheekbones and full lips. Her chin came down into a little point and her wide eyes gave her face a look of innocence.

The maid dashed toward him with her chomping jaw, aiming for his shoulder. Those razor-sharp teeth sliced the skin.

"Aahhh! What the hell did you do that for?"

The maid smiled happily at him.

"That fucking hurt," he griped.

She stared with her devilish grin.

Was this some form of mermaid play? For foke's sake, they were brutal.

"Can you help get me back to the island?" he asked.

She blinked at him. No answer.

"I'm not completing the challenge." He'd get to El Corazón, share his news, and by the time Shane arrived, it would be too late for him to throw a wrench in anything. "And just in case anything happens to me along the way, I think giving you the sacred water will heal you."

The maid shook her head.

"You don't believe me?" he said, barely treading water and out of breath.

She shrugged.

"Well, there's only one way to know for sure. We have to get back and try it."

Whoever this maid was, Roen would save her first. She was an angel who'd rescued him from death and opened his eyes. Because of her, El Corazón was now only minutes away, and Roen would finally see justice done.

Floating on his back, Roen tried to relax his cramped muscles to make the exhausted maid's work less difficult. He was a large man, not designed to reduce drag in the water, and her pace had slowed to a tenth of what it was.

"Fucking sharks," he heard the maid mumble in a gravelly voice.

Roen opened his eyes at the precise moment something bumped him hard from below.

Godfokingdammit. They were both so weak.

The maid pushed him from behind, smacking his back with her tail. "Go, merman."

"No. We'll fight it together." Their chances were better if they ganged up on it. Alone, they had no chance.

"You go!" the maid barked.

"No, I won't leave you—"

The maid smacked him with her long black tail in the back again. "Go. You save them. I fight shark. Hungry anyway."

Roen looked at the creature, who kept ducking her head beneath the water, watching for the shark.

Her head popped up. "I am one. They are many."

"I don't think I can make it," he said.

"One mile. You can," she replied.

The shark's fin popped from the water, heading straight toward them.

"Go!" she screamed and dove into the water, swimming to intercept the large predator.

Roen wanted to stay and protect her. Everything in his gut told him not to leave this creature who'd saved him. But she was right; she was one and there were many to save.

Bobbing in the rough waters, Roen filled his lungs with air and began swimming. Where the strength came from, he didn't know.

A loud howl filled the air. He caught a glimpse of the mermaid shooting from the water, the shark snapping at her tail. The maid dove under and then shot up again. This time the shark caught her tailfin, and the two disappeared beneath the surface in a tangle of teeth and blood.

Roen's heart cried out for her. He could only pray she'd survive. She deserved her life back. *And so do the other thousands.*

He swam with everything he had, and when he finally spotted the golden shore, his heart filled with hope. *Only half a mile more. Think of Liv. Think of seeing her again. Think of her smile and warmth.* Everything he now knew meant they could be together.

Roen kept his head down, imagining that each stroke and kick pulled him closer to Liv.

Almost to the shore, Lyle emerged from the tree line and ran to retrieve him from the waves. "I knew you would return, brother." He wrapped Roen's arm around his shoulder for support.

"How did you know?" Roen panted his words. His entire body shivered violently and his feet and hands had gone completely numb.

God, I hate the foking ocean.

"Because you hate the ocean," Lyle replied. "You're not about to die in it."

Roen made a shallow laugh while Lyle deposited him in the warm sand to sit. Roen had made it, and now it was time to gather the men and make things right.

CHAPTER EIGHTEEN

Roen had not wanted to drink anymore of that goddamned water, but he'd been far too weak to fight off Holden and Lyle when they pinned him to the tile floor in Holden's kitchen.

"You will drink it, Roen," Lyle had said. "You've come too far to die now, and Holden says you have hypothermia."

"Listen to your little brother." Holden had grunted while prying open Roen's mouth. "And stop moving around; you'll make me spill it."

Apparently, the island had kept her word and turned on the spigot after Roen and Shane left; then the water miraculously stopped again a few hours ago.

She knows what's coming.

Luckily, Holden had been smart to stockpile what he could, filling every bottle, jar, mug, and pot with water. Like the island or not, when faced with a fatal injury or condition, most people would choose to live. Which is why Roen finally gave in and drank.

Now healed, Roen asked four of their strongest to catch a maid and bring her to the hall, before having the bell rung.

The men poured in and crowded anxiously around him and Lyle. No doubt, everyone felt shocked as hell to see him.

Roen held up his hands to silence the excited voices.

"How did you beat Shane here?" Jason asked the moment the other voices died down.

Roen crossed his arms over his chest. "I did not finish the challenge for a reason I will explain in a moment. First, I must ask everyone to declare your connection to the island severed."

The room echoed with loud voices questioning his demand.

Roen waved his hands in the air. "To show you proof without her interruption, you must do it. And if I'm right, you will see I've found a way to break the death grip she has over everyone, and that your women, all of them, can be brought back. Starting right now."

That got their attention.

"Anyone who does not wish to do as he's asked may leave," Lyle said.

No one did.

"Good," Roen said. "Now look into your hearts and silently tell her she is no longer welcome here."

The ground shook violently beneath them, and the men began screaming, clasping their hands over their eyes in agony.

Roen repeated, "Shut her out! Tell her to go! The pain will cease if you shut her out." It was a gamble, but he was proof, wasn't he? The island had not touched him.

One by one, the men shook their heads and stood up straight. Roen almost felt like a fool. All along, the solution had been right there. So damned obvious.

Just then, four men stormed in, carrying a wriggling black mass with a thick cloth bag over its head and claws tied behind her back. Roen immediately felt pained thinking of the maid who'd saved him, saved them all, really.

"Move aside!" Lyle commanded.

The room watched in silent angst while the men placed the maid on the floor in front of them and removed the bag. The mermaid snapped her sharp teeth like a crocodile and hissed like a snake.

"Hold her steady," Roen ordered and then uncapped the bottle he held in his hand.

She wiggled her head from side to side while Roen managed to pour some of the water in. It immediately had a calming effect. He poured a little more, and this time, the maid drank it up.

Roen stepped back, praying he hadn't miscalculated. The minutes ticked by, but the maid lay there, dazed.

Nothing happened.

How could I have been wrong? I must've missed something.

The men exchanged glances—some frustrated, some confused, some angry.

The air filled with anguish. No. *This can't be…* He'd failed. Failed.

Lyle patted him on the back. "It's all right, brother. You've freed all of us in this room. We'll figure out the rest."

That wasn't good enough. Without their women, they would never truly be free.

Roen's legs shook with despair. *I failed them. I failed them.*

It was the one thing he feared most in life after failing to save Lyle and his mother. Yes, Lyle ended up being alive, but Roen hadn't been there during those critical moments—when those boys in Glasgow put Lyle in the hospital for months. Lyle had only been eight, and himself not much older, and he'd run away the moment the kids began throwing rocks. He'd left his little brother to die. What sort of person did that? And later, after they and their mother had run from their father to the United States, Roen failed Lyle again. Because their father always tracked them down. Did Roen lift a finger to get Lyle away from that madman or his mother, who wasn't right in the head, either? No. He'd felt too damned worried about himself when he could've done something—called the police, told neighbors or teachers, or even run away and taken Lyle with him. Instead, he'd done nothing, and Lyle eventually ended up here, something that might've happened regardless, but that wasn't the point. Roen hadn't even tried. As for his mother, she'd done her best. Now he knew that the separation from their father had driven her mad; meanwhile being mated to such a madman, knowing what was to come for her children, had broken her heart. Literally.

Now he'd failed at this. What would be next? Would he fail Liv, too?

"Roen!" someone called out.

Roen looked at the maid and could scarcely believe what he saw: a naked woman, petite and blonde, lying on the floor, sleeping. Her skin looked like a Dalmatian's, white with black spots that faded one by one.

Jason rushed forward and dropped to his knees, weeping and clutching the sleeping woman's hand over his heart.

Roen released a breath, and it was so much more than relief. He wanted to fall to his knees and weep alongside Jason and thank the heavens or the spirits of their ancestors or whomever watched over him.

"It's over," he whispered, holding back his own tears of joy. "It's foking over."

They were all going to be free. And once they were, he'd be done with this place forever and ready to move on. *With Liv.*

The rest of the day, Roen and the men worked at setting up nets and traps to ensnare the maids, using anything they had for bait: fish, meat from their freezers, even cookies and candy. So far, they'd caught twenty just this evening. Meanwhile, he'd sent Lyle and a group of men in search of the elders, who were nowhere to be found. Were they hiding from him? Or fearing the end to a way of life that had existed for thousands of years? He didn't know, and it didn't matter. He need only focus on getting the maids transformed and then getting everyone who wanted to leave off the island.

In the case of the old bitch, no one had heard or felt anything for hours, and the walls of the cavern were bone dry. She had to have realized her reign of cruelty was over, and that now they held the cards. She would want their protection, and if they chose to give it, he would make her pay. The time of cowering and bending over was done.

Roen helped two men administer water to a feisty fifteen-foot-long maid. Holden walked into the great hall with a worried look on his face, his flaming red hair a mess.

"What's the matter?" Roen asked.

Holden leaned in close to whisper into Roen's ear. "Some of the women are waking up now, but they are not themselves."

Roen let out a breath and rubbed his brow. "What do you mean?"

"They don't remember who they are."

Roen's sense of triumph momentarily soured. "Do you think they might remember eventually?"

Holden shook his head. "I don't know. But I thought I should tell everyone so they're not shocked."

Roen nodded. "Yes, please let the men know. And tell them not to give up hope yet." The priority, at this point, however, was getting the women back and reunited with their mates, for those that had any still alive. He estimated that roughly half of the men wore black—one hundred. If there were thousands of mermaids out in those waters, it meant the majority of their men had passed away. Breaking the news to those women would not be easy. *Maybe they won't remember, a blessing in disguise again.*

"Roen?" Roen and Holden turned their heads to find Jason standing there with red eyes. "I wanted to thank you—" the large man whisked away a tear "—the first woman you brought in was Amelia. I never thought I'd see her again."

Roen felt a small spark of satisfaction. "Has she woken up yet?"

"No, but I've already heard the news. I don't care if she doesn't remember me. Her heart will remember."

Roen gave Jason a pat on his bare shoulder. "You're welcome."

"I don't deserve your mercy, Roen," Jason fell to his knees, weeping, "but I beg you to forgive me."

"Of course I forgive you. I am not—"

"She broke our most sacred law." Jason continued sobbing. "I had no choice but to follow Naylor's orders. I'm sorry, Roen. I am sorry."

Roen's heart clenched into a tight knot. "What are you talking about, Jason?"

"No one told you?" Holden said, his red face fading to a pale white.

Roen shook his head. He almost didn't want to know, and his mind had already produced the worst possible scenario. *Liv…*

"What did they do to Liv?" Roen asked.

"She's dead." Jason sobbed.

Did he say she's dead? "No," Roen argued. "Lyle put her on a plane, her and Dana."

Holden shook his head. "I heard them speaking after you left. Shane and his men attacked Lyle. Dana got on the plane, but not Liv."

Roen couldn't believe his ears. Why hadn't Lyle said anything? He lunged at Holden, throwing him to the floor.

Holden raised his palms. "I didn't know. It was Naylor, Shane, and his men—but they were within their rights. Liv broke the law. She told the landlovers about our water and where we are. Now there are a hundred ships looking for our island."

"You sons of bitches." Roen spun in a circle. "Where is Liv?" He glanced at Jason still falling to pieces on the floor. He pulled back his foot, ready to break the man in two, when Lyle appeared out of nowhere, knocking Roen down.

"No, brother," Lyle yelled. "You cannot kill him. No law has been broken."

Fueled by rage, Roen was on his feet. "Why didn't you tell me?"

Lyle got up and held his hands in the air. "Because I knew you'd kill me when you learned I'd failed you."

"So you're a coward?" Roen seethed, losing his mind.

"No. I merely wanted to spend another day with you before I died. That, and I'd really hoped Shane would return so I could rip out his throat."

This can't be happening. This can't foking be happening. "She's not dead," Roen argued. "You're all lying to me. Where is she?"

Lyle's eyes filled with tears. It was a first. "She was fed to the maids."

No. No. No. "Is that true, you piece of shit?" Roen seethed at Jason.

Jason slowly got to his feet and stared at the floor. "Yes."

"Which beach? Where?" Roen asked, feeling the world cave in on him.

Jason pointed to the beach about a half mile south.

Roen turned and sprinted for his life.

Why? Why did she tell the landlovers about their water? *No. It's a lie. She wouldn't do that. She'd never do that.*

Roen's heart pounded and his lungs burned as he ducked branches and ran as fast as his body permitted.

"Liv!" he screamed the moment he stepped foot onto the dark beach. "Liv!"

He jumped into the water and swam out, the salt water stinging his eyes. He stopped, treading water. "Liv! Where are you?" *She can't be dead. She can't be.*

"Tell me where she is, you foking monsters." He pounded his fists into the water, ready to throttle the truth from the first maid who popped her head up.

Not one came.

Roen's entire body went into shock. Somewhere in the back of his mind, he knew this was coming. He knew he would lose her. And for what? This place?

Roen's soul ripped down the cold middle.

He'd been thinking about being the hero and sacrificing himself to save everyone. But if Shane and Naylor had been a part of this, they'd known even before the challenge had begun. They killed her and then hoped Roen would die, too.

"Well, I'm not *foking* dead! You *foking* hear me? I'm going to kill you!" Rage took the place of Roen's despair. He would hunt Naylor, hunt Shane's men, including Jason, and once Shane showed up, he'd tear out his heart. *Then I'll sink this whole foking island to the bottom of the ocean.*

Roen emerged from the waves and released a war cry filled with his contempt for the very air he breathed. It wasn't supposed to end like this. He loved Liv. He loved her, and they'd never even had a chance to be happy for one goddamned day.

I will kill those fucking bastards. Roen stormed toward his home, making a mental list of which weapons he'd collect and who he'd kill first. He tripped and fell flat on his face in the sand. He quickly flipped onto his ass and caught a glimpse of a black form lying on the beach, its long flowing tail swishing with the ebb and flow of the small waves.

He moved closer. Was she dead? Cautiously, he moved his ear to its mouth and felt a soft breath against his ear.

Is this my angel? In the darkness, he couldn't see much.

He scooped the unconscious maid in his arms, noticing how his heart seemed to recognize her.

Like the times you've held...

He stopped in his tracks and stared down at the thing, his eyes reaching and pushing through the darkness of night to catch any details. Could it be?

"Liv?" he whispered.

She had been thrown to the maids for food. They would've torn her up, wouldn't they? But his heart still felt their connection. The bond between them wasn't gone. *She's not dead.* So was this Liv? Or was his mind trying to force a hope into being because he couldn't handle the truth?

The maid gasped in his arms and made an agonized howling sound.

"Hang on. Hang on." Roen walked at a brisk pace, careful not to make any injuries worse.

Minutes later, Roen entered the great hall, where everyone still worked in small teams, bringing in the maids and giving them water. Other men saw to clothing the women or getting them to cottages where Holden could tend to them properly.

"Someone bring me water," Roen yelled. With the torchlight inside the hall, he now saw a deep gash on the maid's thigh and another across her abdomen. No doubt about it, this was his maid, his savior. The one who'd thrown herself at a shark to save him.

"You're going to be okay," he whispered.

One of the men brought water. Roen poured a few tiny drops into the creature's mouth. "Please be okay. Please be okay," he chanted under his breath while thinking, *Please be Liv. Please be Liv.*

He poured a little more water and watched it disappear down the creature's mouth. Nothing seemed to be happening. He held up her head and gave her more. This time she drank a few good gulps.

"That's right. Drink it down," he said. With every sip, her wounds closed up a little more and the bleeding stopped. Sadly, while he sat there with the maid's head in his lap, stroking the tendrils of the long and strange black hair, no transformation occurred.

"Please, tell me how long it's been taking for the women to change back?" Roen asked the man standing over him who'd brought the water. Roen couldn't remember his name—*Draco or Darrin?*

"A few minutes. Why?"

"And how much water did you give them?" Roen stared at the maid in his arms.

"I don't know. A cup maybe? How much have you given that one?"

"An entire bottle," Roen replied.

"That's strange."

Roen stared down at her face, now seeing those lovely details masked by the skin of a horrid monster. "No," he said, his voice cracking. "It's not strange. Liv is resistant to the water."

Roen now knew that the bite of a merman transformed a woman into these creatures. It might be possible the maids' bites carried the same venom or substance. Had the maids bitten Liv and not killed her? Or maybe she fought back and got away.

My Liv. My damned fearless Liv. You probably kicked the crap out of one of them.

He stroked her forehead. "We'll figure out how to bring you back. I promise."

The maid's golden yellow eyes slowly opened, and after several moments of staring, the corners of her black lips curled into a content smile.

CHAPTER NINETEEN

Roen had the fish tank in the library cleared out for Liv, who now rested peacefully inside. At least, he hoped it was her. Everything in his heart told him so. And because she'd healed from her wounds, but hadn't transformed back even after two gallons of water, there wasn't much room left for doubt.

Roen glanced at the tank worriedly. *Try to remember, you thought she'd died.* At a minimum, this left the door open for hope. *Still, I can't stand seeing her like this.* He felt like his beautiful mate and everything she'd once been had vanished. Looking at her, he no longer felt those deep emotions, although he still felt love in his heart. Perhaps her soul, the essence of who she was, had already moved on. It was what many of the men believed, and it would explain why the maids they'd brought back couldn't remember who they were.

Roen rubbed his face and let out an anguished breath. As much as he wanted to focus on Liv, they'd hit a new wall. No more water. Again.

They'd spilled half their supply while fighting the maids to drink and some of the men had administered more than necessary. By morning, Roen received word the maids were flocking to shore on their own. Why? No one knew, but Roen had to make the call—keep working until they ran out or stop and figure out how to stretch the supply.

"Keep going," he'd ordered. With so much water wasted, they'd run out anyway and have to face the problem of getting more. "At least a few more men will have their mates back today." They'd proceeded to catch as many maids as possible until the shores were overrun. The beaches now looked like the mating grounds for sea lions, shiny black bodies with tails on every inch of shoreline. There was no way off the island.

Worse yet, Roen had confirmed hundreds of landlover ships sailing in their direction, looking for the "Fountain of Youth." Liv's doctor had sent a water sample to a laboratory in Ketchikan, and an employee leaked the news. With hard data. The part he couldn't wrap his head around was how the island's location had gotten out.

So now, the men were no longer being controlled, but they had no means to bring back the rest of the women without that goddamned water. *One more goddamned hurdle among an ocean of many.*

He'd considered threatening the island with vacating, leaving her to live out her nightmare of being taken over by landlovers, but if anyone found this place and took it over, the mermen's hopes of rescuing Liv or the remaining maids would be done. The humans would either contaminate the island—like the legends said—or they would destroy everything looking for the water. Either way, the island had once again put them in the position of protecting her. They needed her.

I bet she's laughing her ass off right now.

Roen picked up his phone from the desk he'd brought into the library to be near Liv and dialed Phil, who picked up on the first ring. "Ro? Where the hell have you been? I've left twenty messages."

Roen groaned. Phil only used his nickname when there was bad news coming.

"I've been tied up. What's the matter?"

"I've done everything I can, Roen. I've called every senator, judge, I've filed petitions, I even tried to get a meeting with the goddamned president. No one will touch this territory thing."

"Why not? It's my foking land," Roen barked.

"The United States can't go around staking claims on properties in international waters without establishing who occupies it. What if there are bunch of Russians living there? Or French? The U.S. doesn't want to get into a war over a damned island."

Foke. At this point, did it matter if he told Phil the location of the island? Within days, they'd be found out anyway. "It's my island and the people who live here won't contest that." *Not entirely.* "I'll email you the location." Roen rubbed his forehead. "But please hurry. We're about to be overrun by a lot of unwelcomed guests."

"Roen, by coincidence, is this the same island everyone's talking about in the news? The place with a Fountain of Youth?"

"Yes." Roen sighed exasperatedly.

"Holy shit. No wonder you wanted to keep it secret."

"There is no fountain, Phil. It's only an island," he lied. "With some rare species." *The rarest.*

"I'll get to work, but it'll take time."

"We're out of time. Do what you can, please." *Before this turns into a bloodbath.*

Roen hung up the phone and a light tapping sound caught his attention. He turned his head toward the tank, where the maid stared at him with her bright golden eyes. She flashed her set of sharp teeth.

Roen's heart sank further into that deep hole. His beautiful Liv had been turned into this creature. If he managed to transform her back, she might not remember him.

He stood and placed his palms flat on the glass, staring longingly at the strange animal with sleek black skin and a long tail. "I miss you, Liv. I miss your smartass mouth. I miss your face. I miss holding you. Please, at least tell me you know who I am."

She placed her palm against the glass, matching the splay of his fingers with hers. Then she licked her lips, her gaze turning hungry.

"You want to eat me. And not in a good way, I'm guessing," he said.

She made a sour face and then shook her head.

He stepped back and dropped his hand. "I'll try to get you some food." They'd run out of that, too. Everything they had had been used for bait, and the men couldn't get anywhere near the boats to fish—the shores of the island were completely overrun with hungry, snapping, hissing mermaids. If only he had a plane, but Edward—the pilot—wasn't answering his cell. Worst of all, the plane carrying Dana never reached the airport in Wrangell. He'd already checked.

Roen ran his hands over his face. Everything was falling apart around him. *Why can't I catch a foking break?* A punishment for his human sins, perhaps.

"Brother." Lyle stood in the doorway of the library, his face void of real emotion.

Roen didn't have to ask; he knew it meant more bad news. *An endless pile of shit.*

"We've looked everywhere. There are no signs of the elders, so we can only assume they left the island," Lyle said.

Like rats jumping ship. This place really was about to sink, but at least he had his brother at his side. Without him, he wouldn't have survived this long.

"Lyle, did you really believe I would kill you?" Roen asked.

Lyle shrugged his husky shoulders. "It was a strong possibility."

"Why would you think that?"

"I caused you immeasurable suffering." Lyle's green eyes focused on the pile of papers sitting on Roen's desk.

"Yes. You did. Fifteen years of it, to be exact." Roen sat in his leather chair and leaned back.

"No. I meant failing to get Liv off the island." His eyes flashed to the watchful mermaid in the tank. "But now that you mention the other point, I suppose that, too, is worthy of a little anger." Pain and regret flourished in Lyle's face. He was a large man—seven feet tall with enormous muscles and scar-covered skin—but the man standing before him looked like a child desperate for forgiveness.

"Shane and his men blindsided you, it's not your fault Liv was taken," Roen said. "All that other stuff is in the past now. Where it belongs. I'm sorry I brought it up."

Lyle shook his head. "I owe you the truth."

"You don't owe me anything. You're here by my side now, and that's all I could ask for."

"No. You need to know what happened. We may not get another chance."

Roen released a breath and nodded his consent. He could see in Lyle's eyes that his brother needed to get this off his chest.

Lyle walked toward the tank and began speaking to Roen, but his eyes were set on the maid, who seemed fixated by her own swishing tail. "When the previous leader died, father came to see me. He told me everything—about the island, about him and Mom, and about our bloodline. He said you were too weak to rule and that you wouldn't stand a chance, so it was up to me to step in."

Roen dropped his head. "Honestly, I already guessed it was something like that."

Lyle's deep voice quieted. "That wasn't the part I'm ashamed of. I lied to you, Roen. I didn't come here to spare you from having to lead. I came here because he told me that one day you might show up on this island, and if you did, I'd get the honor of killing you."

Lyle's words deeply wounded him. What man wouldn't feel hurt knowing his own father thought him weak and his brother wanted to kill him?

Roen leaned forward in his chair, resting his elbows on the desk while the heavy weight of Lyle's words sank in.

"I agreed, Roen. I hated you for failing to protect me. I hated you since that day those kids put me in the hospital. I hated you for telling me our mother would live. I especially hated you for not protecting me from our father and this place. I felt like every time I needed you, you weren't there, and I looked forward to the day I'd face you and squeeze the life from your body."

Roen lifted his brows and blew out a breath. Lyle's sharp words felt like a hundred little knives being shoved into his gut repeatedly. Only because he felt the same way. "Well, I did fail you. And I can't go back and undo it, but I'll never do it again. I promise."

"No need for an apology, brother. I finally see things differently now that I've closed my heart to the island. You've made me realize she caused our pain. She told our father what to do."

"Yes, but he listened," Roen argued.

"Because he was the weak one, not you. He had the chance to save our mother with the island's water, and he didn't do it because the island told him not to. He already had two sons and couldn't have more, so she was of no use—that's what the island said to him."

"How do you know all this?" Roen asked.

"I was there when he died. He killed himself—said the guilt was too much and threw himself to the maids."

"Like the goddamned coward that he was." Roen's anger, resentment, and despair bubbled to the surface. How much more could he endure?

"Yes. He was a coward. And perhaps he feared your strength and what it might do to the way of life here. But the island… I think she was drawn to you. She's drawn to strength and determination. It's irresistible to her. Almost like she feeds off of it."

The maid hit the glass with her knuckles and began swishing frantically back and forth in the tank, pointing to her throat.

"Sorry," Roen said. "She's hungry."

"I know how she feels. I haven't eaten in two days, but none of that matters now." Lyle squared his shoulders. "Roen, whatever happens next, I want you to know I'm proud to have been your brother. And now you need to come outside," he added.

"Why?" Roen asked hesitantly.

"I need to show you something."

Goddammit, what now? "Just tell me."

"It's better if you see for yourself."

Roen ran his hands through his hair. Whatever it was couldn't be worse than what they already faced.

"Stay in there." Roen pointed to the maid. With his luck, he'd come back and find she'd eaten one of his men.

The maid popped her head from the top of the tank. "Eat! Eat! Island eat!" Her voice came out sounding like a cross between a wolf's howl and seal's bark.

Roen groaned. One more goddamned thing to worry about. A ravenous mermaid mate.

He followed Lyle out the front door, wondering what more could possibly go wrong.

Once outside, Roen immediately noticed how the late evening sky seemed flat, pale blue on one side and light gray on the other. No orange. No electric blue. Just a plain old sky.

Lyle pointed to the trees. "Look at them. Look at their tops."

They'd browned, like old dried-out Christmas trees.

"What's happening to them?" Roen asked.

"I think the island is dying. Now look at your hands, Roen." Lyle held out his own palm, revealing patches of black skin.

Roen stuck out his right hand and noticed he too had pea-sized spots. When he looked closer, he saw a slight texture to them. "What is it?"

"I guess we're dying, too."

"Foking hell." Roen dropped his hands. "Either that, or we're changing into bloody mermen."

Shane stared at the dark-haired beauty sleeping on the bed, fantasizing over every inch. Oh, the things he was going to do to that smart mouth and those heart-shaped lips, to that creamy skin and sweet-smelling body.

And I'm going to enjoy every moment.

He'd sold his goddamned soul and betrayed everyone who trusted him to finally get what he wanted. Fuck them all because his blackened heart wept with joy.

Liv groaned softly in the bed and stretched her arms over her head. "Mmmm…"

"Feeling well rested, landlover?" he said. "I had to give you quite a bit of sedatives while the sacred water healed your many wounds. It took a lot of time, and I'm sorry for that, but the maids had to make it look convincing."

Liv sat up, her wide brown eyes darting around the room. "Shane? Where am I?"

He leaned forward, planting his elbows on his knees. "You're in my home. *Your* home. On my private island."

Her eyes continued surveying the well-appointed room—only the best of the best for his comfort. Lush, rich upholstery, gas fireplace, balcony overlooking the ocean. Oh, yes. And Liv. She would bring him endless nights of comfort.

"Shane?" she said with a shaky voice. "Where's Roen?"

He stood and pushed up the sleeves of his thick cream-colored sweater. It felt good to wear clothes again, especially jeans. “Roen? Oh, he’s dead along with the rest of those weak, disloyal traitors.” At least, they would be soon. “But you and I have been given a great honor, Liv, one I think we’ll both enjoy.”

He could hear the frantic pounding of her heart inside her chest, but he’d anticipated this reaction. With time, however, she’d see this was meant to be.

“What are you talking about, Shane?”

“You and I will repopulate my race with men bigger, stronger, and far more loyal than those I left behind.” He sat next to her and ran the tip of his finger across her trembling jaw. “You,” he whispered, “are going to give me many sons. Any more questions?”

“Yeah,” she said, stabbing him with her angry eyes. “What’s the best way to kill a merman?”

TO BE CONTINUED…

NOTE FROM AUTHOR

Hi All!

So what do you think? Are they dying or becoming…mua-ha-ha-ha…mermen? And who the hell is inside Roen's fish tank? And will Liv finally get to kill Shane? Hmmm…*crosses fingers.* LOL. While you're thinking about it, here are some fun pics to check out of the characters and places in the book:

www.pinterest.com/mimijeanromance/mermen/

Anyway, I am SUPER-DUPER sorry to make everyone wait for part 3 (coming LATE NOV. 2015), but I needed to hit pause and finish up IMMORTAL MATCHMAKERS, INC. (my NEW Accidentally Yours spin off—yay CIMIL!!), and readers have been very patient for that. I'm also working on my next installment of the Happy Pants Café Series (Summer 2016—so excited!).

If you'd like to know exactly when MerCiless is coming, sign up for my monthly newsletter (exclusive sneak peeks and monthly giveaways!) so you don't miss it:

http://goo.gl/0CrVMG or go to www.mimijean.net.

AND DON'T MISS OUT on Mermen SWAG! If you'd like a free signed bookmark, shoot me your address (mimi@mimijean.net). If you write a cool REVIEW, PLEASE mention it as I usually have extra goodies as thank yous! (My supplies are limited, so do hurry!)

FINALLY, King fans, be SURE to check out the Up and Coming Releases. (COVER REVEAL on the next pages!!) Mermen fans…ditto!

HAPPY READING!

Hugs,

Mimi

Acknowledgments

Once again, ARRRGGGH-gargle-gargle (mermaid speak for "thank you") to Team Mimi for playing this round of the "Hey, what do you think?", "Is it ready?", and "Rush, rush, rush." Kylie, Dali, Ally, Latoya, Pauline, Su, Jan, and Stef, you are all rock stars. Couldn't do this without you folks!

MerCiless COMING November 2015

Book 3, The Mermen Trilogy

MACK. COMING SPRING 2016

His truth won't break you.
It will tear your heart to pieces.

IMMORTAL MATCHMAKERS, INC.
COMING AUGUST 2015

BECAUSE…dysfunctional immortals need love, too.

ANDRUS

Once the most powerful immortal assassin ever to exist, this demigod now spends his days pining for the girl who got away: Helena. Doesn't help that he's also Helena's full-time nanny slash bodyguard. But now that the apocalypse is over and her husband, the vampire general, has returned home for good, it's time to move on.

But can Andrus let go of the woman he secretly loves?

Cimil, Goddess of the Underworld and owner of Immortal Matchmakers, Inc., knows the solution is finding another gal. The right gal. But getting a woman to date this callous, unrefined, coldhearted warrior will prove to be the biggest challenge of her existence. Good thing they're in L.A.

When aspiring actress Sadie Townsend finds herself one week away from being thrown out on the street, the call from her agent is like a gift from heaven. But when she learns the job is teaching the world's biggest barbarian how to act like a gentleman, she wonders if she shouldn't have asked for more money. He's vulgar, uncaring, and rougher around the edges than a serrated bread knife. He's also sexy, fierce, and undeniably tormented.

Will Sadie help him overcome his past, or will she find her heart hopelessly trapped by a man determined to self-destruct?

KING TRILOGY AUDIOBOOK

King Trilogy Available in Audiobook

KING'S – March 31, 2015

KING FOR A DAY – April 21, 2015

KING OF ME – May 12, 2015

Find Buy Links at:

mimijean.net/king_trilogy_books.html

ABOUT THE AUTHOR

Mimi Jean Pamfiloff is a *New York Times* & *USA Today* best-selling author of Paranormal and Contemporary Romance. Her books have been #1 genre sellers around the world. Both traditionally and independently published, Mimi has sold over 500,000 books since publishing her first title in 2012, and she plans to spontaneously combust once she hits the one million mark. Although she obtained her international MBA and worked for over 15 years in the corporate world, she believes that it's never too late to come out of the romance closet and follow your dream.

When not screaming at her computer or hosting her very inappropriate radio show (*Man Candy Show* on Radioslot.com), Mimi spends time with her two pirates in training, her loco-for-the-chili-pepper Mexican hubby, and her rat terrier, DJ Princess Snowflake, in the San Francisco Bay Area.

She continues to hope that her books will inspire a leather pants comeback (for men) and that she might make you laugh when you need it most.

Sign up for Mimi's mailing list
for giveaways and new release news!

LEARN MORE:

mailto: mimi@mimijean.net

www.mimijean.net

twitter.com/MimiJeanRomance

http://radioslot.com/show/mancandyshow/

www.facebook.com/MimiJeanPamfiloff

19784822R00157

Made in the USA
Middletown, DE
04 May 2015